ALL YOU CAN KILL

PASHA MALLA

Coach House Books, Toronto

Published with the generous assistance of the Canada Council for the Arts and the Ontario Arts Council. Coach House Books also acknowledges the support of the Government of Canada through the Canada Book Fund and the Government of Ontario through the Ontario Book Publishing Tax Credit.

LIBRARY AND ARCHIVES CANADA CATALOGUING IN PUBLICATION

Title: All you can kill / Pasha Malla.
Names: Malla, Pasha, author
Description: First edition.
Identifiers: Canadiana (print) 20240445732 | Canadiana (ebook) 20240445740 | ISBN 9781552454862 (softcover) | ISBN 9781770568181 (PDF) | ISBN 9781770568174 (EPUB)
Subjects: LCGFT: Novels.
Classification: LCC PS8626.A449 A79 2024 | DDC C813/.6—dc23

All You Can Kill is available as an ebook: ISBN 978 1 77056 817 4 (EPUB), ISBN 978 1 77056 818 1 (PDF)

Purchase of the print version of this book entitles you to a free digital copy. To claim your ebook of this title, please email sales@chbooks.com with proof of purchase. (Coach House Books reserves the right to terminate the free digital download offer at any time.)

He did not believe, and yet he admitted the supernatural, for how was it possible to deny, on this very earth, the mystery that arises within us, around us, in our homes, on the streets – everywhere, when you think about it? It was far too facile to dismiss those invisible extrahuman relationships or to attribute to chance, which is itself indecipherable, unforeseen events, misfortunes and coincidences. Did not a casual encounter often decide the entire life of a person? What was love, or any incomprehensible, formative influence? And, finally, was not the most unsettling enigma of all that of money?

– Joris-Karl Huysmans, *Là-Bas*

One

Imagine, if you will:

Two people floating through the air. A man and a woman. Clutching each other, bodies pressed like lips in a grimace, up and out and over the land.

The woman is one K. Sohail, dressed in the traditional attire of the security guard: beige uniform, peaked cap, sneakers, ring of keys on her hip.

The man is me.

Ask not how we got here. Only picture us and believe. Your faith keeps us aloft, probably.

Who's clutching whom? In a clutch is there always a clutcher and a clutchee? Can there be mutual clutching? Or perhaps it happens in turns: for a bit you do the clutching, then you leaven your grip and brace to be clutched. For a clutch is not the harmonious yin and yang of a lovers' embrace, with two people twined like paisleys. A clutch is desperate! And desperate is how I felt, buoyed aloft over a patchwork of farmland stitched with grey threads of bitumen: the farms, the roads, the earth below.

Though that makes our flight, such as it was, sound grandiose – 'a bird's view from its eyes.' In fact we floated a mere fifty feet above the ground, fairly modest as air travel goes, especially compared to the astral, cloud-rending propulsions of the jumbo jet, buzzard, or freewheeling balloon. So, yes, below us were farms and roads, but were I to claim that from our altitude the cars looked like ants, or the sheep like maggots on the gangrenous hides of rotting corpses, i.e., the grassy hills, I would be lying. In fact they looked exactly like cars, driving steadily to home or work or masseuse as we floated past, and sheep. What did we look like to them, I wondered, these floating fugitives with legs dangling limply – her sneakers, my stockinged feet – our two bodies fused as one? Weird?

Perhaps. Due to a colonial upbringing as stiff-lipped as a rictus, I am not so fluent in the more common intimacies of our species: clutching, yes, but also hugging, cuddling, snuggling, nuzzling, nestling, nesting, partnered dancing, partnered prancing, canoodling, commingling, doing the hustle and/or bustle, intercourses dialogic and genital, a gay foxtrot, a freaky jive, how's-your-father, my-father's-fine-how's-yours, the hokey-pokey, the oozy-poozy, the horizontal polka, the conventionally vertical polka, squished sardines, annihilated anchovies, lobster rolls, kissing, smooching, pashing, Frenching, Swedish massage, finishing moves, happy endings, sadly pre-emptive endings, footsies, footjobs, handjobs, nosejobs, four-on-the-floor, a table for two, sixty-niners, one-on-one, three-a-side, the old one-two, the old in-out, congress, sex, love, etc., and so forth.

Though I must admit that I was warmed by K. Sohail's body. Our flight felt nice. And while the wind, undeniably, buffeted us along – and certainly your faith, gentle reader, couldn't hurt – it seemed that we were keeping *each other* airborne. That our embrace engendered some sort of power or energy or spooky spell that propelled us through the (low) sky, and, as if we were dreaming the same dream, to release each other would snap us irrevocably, tragically awake and send us careening head-long to earth.

So it was just good to be held, and to hold someone, for a while. Also descent seemed scary – the sputter, the pause, the plummet. Into what? A quagmire, a house fire, a swamp of horny toads; we could land anywhere. Yet for now, or then, on we sailed as the farms below became forests, and then plains, and the minutes became hours, and I became hungry, and then famished. We'd been flying through several mealtimes, at least.

Behind us the sun began to sink, and our shadows yawned over the earth in its fading rays as we found ourselves, bellies gurgling, reaching the limits of the land: red cliffs, brown scrub, and finally yellow beach onto which the sea churned and receded with a gasp like spent laughter. As if the surf were mocking our hunger. As if it heard the peptic orches-trations of our starving and guffawed. And then we crossed over that sandy boundary marking the terrestrial plane, and beneath our feet was only water.

The wind pushed us out. The dinner hour passed. The sun went down. The sky purpled and blackened, like a blistering skin. The stars emerged glitzily. My gut groaned, as did K. Sohail's – like a pair of degenerate lions mewling their sad last breaths to the indifferent savannah. We were travelling low enough that I could smell the sea's fishy buffet; oh for a bite of bass, a nibble of clam!

And still that upward draft carried us offshore, until the land receded – a dark stripe at the horizon, then a haze, and then gone – and all that surrounded us in every direction was the infinite night and that writhing black desert below. The wettest, angriest desert of all, bullied only by the moon. How? Lunar phases, gravity, the poles – that is, not the fair citizens of Poland, but the ends of the earth itself whose magnetism tugs apples from trees – and, soon enough, we feared, K. Sohail and me from the sky.

But for now we were simply out to sea, which clapped and sizzled darkly beneath us as we drifted overtop and the sea breeze pushed us on. Exhausted and ravenous, we slept. And woke even hungrier, our mouths cottony and bellies aching, as dawn arrived: the sun nudged over the horizon ahead, spangling the water pink, then orange, and lifted arrogantly into the paling sky.

My god – feed me seaweed, feed me brine. A clot of rancid abalone. Anything!

– Look, said K. Sohail in a parched, crackling voice. And so I looked.

A diversion from our famine: a pod of dolphins frolicked through the waves.

And then a swordfish breached the surface in a great, searing arc.

And then a whale tooted a geyser.

– Look deeper, she said.

Beneath its squalls the sea revealed even wilder astonishments.

Two starfish made sensual love in a tangle of kinky limbs.

A cloud of variegated, fan-shaped fish dithered one way then the other; it was, in truth, exasperating.

A flounder floundered – a platonic specimen indeed.

A shipwreck seethed with all manner of life, including a family of seahorses, trotting haughtily along the current, as demure as monarchs.

Could such a creature be tamed and ridden? By only the surest, tiniest of equestrians, certainly.

Also: a bored turtle, a grinning ray, a sucker-puckered octopus, a walrus with the moustache of a custodial worker and tusks to match, and a feast of shrimp, lobster, crab, mussels, scallops, oysters … A scrumptious smorgasbord! And here we were, without a single pat of butter. My stomach rumbled and crooned. Or was that K. Sohail's? We were pressed so snugly that even our digestive enzymes carolled as one.

– Keep looking, urged K. Sohail, deeper.

Affixed to a bank of coral, knobby and fluorescent as an old drunk's nose, an urchin wobbled and gobbled plankton by the thousand. Yum.

An aardvark, I think – what in god's name was it doing down there? Some ink. A cloud of ink.

All the way down, a fish with a flashlight for a head bumbled along the sea floor, like some hapless miner on the hunt for precious stones.

Deeper still, a leviathan dwelled in the sea's most hellish trench, possibly. (It was very, very dark at those depths; who knew for sure.)

– Look, said K. Sohail again, nodding to the surface: a shark's fin cut the waves like a blade through damp cheese.

And the shark dove, and struck, and ate the flounder!

And the whale ate the shark! In one gulp! Just like that!

Blood frothed and foamed; shark bits spewed through the whale's baleen.

– Nature, I narrated simply.

For a time we were silent, contemplating. But then a new, jealous hunger replaced the old one. My mouth felt fossilized. The sun was a roaring maw. If I didn't consume something soon, I would perish. (We, that is – K. Sohail too.)

But then, again, yet with an upward lilt:

– Look.

She was directing my gaze now to the sky. So I looked up, and where one might expect to observe gulls or winged fish soaring through 'yonder's blue greatness,' I spied a helicopter, bearing down from above with fire and smoke spewing from its tail.

A helicopter!

A helicopter, only two hundred yards away and blatantly struggling. That is if one assumes that the preferred trajectory of any aircraft is upward liftoff, a gentle parabola of flight, then a controlled landing like a breeze-nudged feather settling to rest – and not hurtling headlong toward the ocean in a great ruckus of flame.

Our leisurely drift seemed so sedate compared to how the aircraft lurched and veered, propellors languishing, engines ablaze. Down it went wheeling (anti-clockwise), finally righting itself into a smouldering nosedive – only to crash headlong into the ocean. A massive font of water exploded skyward, great breakers haloed, crashed, hissed, and swept outward. A column of bubbles chortled to the surface. Then these faded too.

We approached the crash site, passing through an acrid wisp of smoke lilting up from the water. I held my breath and peered below. Nothing was visible in the blackly churning sea. Somewhere down there were, presumably, human victims. Passengers, a pilot. Did helicopters have a cabin crew? Were air stewards, or flight attendants, or 'sky waiters,' employed to wheel around a cart of tiny drinks and pretzels?

Wrong to think of food now. And K. Sohail seemed to be trying to free herself from my arms and leap below!

– Wait, I cried, seizing (yes, clutching) her.

– We must save them, she replied, struggling.

– Look around, it's water for miles. You'll only drown. And then where will we be?

Grimly, grudgingly, she relented and returned to my clutch. On we floated, leaving the wreck behind, with nothing in our path once again but the wide-open sea.

– I suppose, she said after a period of calculation, that we can only hope whoever was aboard was roasted to death in the fire or the impact of the crash snapped their necks like breadsticks. Better than drowning, anyway.

This sharp articulation of human tragedy – moreover with that precisely calibrated simile – stilled my hunger. I no longer felt anything. We merely drifted in reverential, stunned silence as the sun ascended and poured its ferocious, scorching light upon us.

Yet – were we sinking? It seemed almost imperceptible, a slight dip easily attributable to air currents. But closer inspection revealed a declining trajectory, as if a ramp laid at our feet were guiding us gradually seaward.

– You feel it too, said K. Sohail.

– Feel?

– We're going down.

Indeed. Whatever power held us aloft was fading. So this was it, I thought, gazing forlornly at the approaching sea: crashed and drowned like a helicopter – at best. At worst, nibbled to death by some prawns.

But then!

– Look, K. Sohail recited mantrically, pointing toward the horizon.

I followed her finger. Peered. Squinted. Was that some stylishly coiffed kraken breaching the surface to feast on our sinking bodies in torrents of spraying gore? No. What I'd taken for the artfully trimmed bangs of a sea monster were in fact palm trees fringing a shoreline.

Blooming out of the water, like some sort of reverse-oasis, appeared an island.

Rarely in life does one occasion upon irrevocable proof of a higher power. But sometimes a coincidence stretches not just the bounds of credulity, but possibility: there is no way to explain, for example, a swarm of bees flying into your bully's mouth before he can smear you, or the impossible serendipity of a perfectly synchronized *jinx*, other than – dare I say it! – the celestial intervention of the gods.

Had the island not materialized at that precise moment, with K. Sohail and I sagging so low over the waves that the salt-spray spritzed our toes, we would surely have drowned. But, miraculously, just as our flight extinguished, some ex-machinal force guided us to dry land. We stumbled, fell to our knees, released each other, and collapsed like a stump hewn in half on the beach.

For a moment I lay upon the sand – sand as white as sugar, but nowhere near as delicious.

– Are you *eating* it? asked K. Sohail.

I laughed loudly and spat secretly. The hunger had returned!

– Well here we are, she said.

I agreed. We'd landed upon a classic 'island desert.' Would this now entail archetypal waiting for rescue, growing wild beards, and finally devouring each other's thigh-meat in the gloomy cannibalism of survival? I hoped not. And considering the divine providence of our landing, I wondered if we ought to perform some act of veneration to whichever god might have lent us a hand. Just to cover our bases.

Was there some ceremony we might perform? A symbolic totem to be fashioned upon the sand? I looked up the beach to the treeline, garnished with ferns and reeds rustling in the sea breeze, for some driftwood or craft supplies with which to fashion an effigy. But my eye caught on an unexpected curiosity: a man-made gap interrupted the foliage.

– Is that a path?

– And a sign, said K. Sohail, standing.

Together we went over to examine it: a wooden placard affixed at waist-height to a stake in the ground. My hunger sang mournfully, hoping the sign would advertise the nearest delicatessen or 'eatery,' or even farm. A menu would be nice!

RETREAT commanded the sign instead, with an arrow pointing into the jungle.

– Retreat? I queried.

K. Sohail shrugged.

I turned back to face the sea. Were we being pursued? No sign of anyone out there, just the boundless, infuriating, glittering waves over which we'd sailed. So a retreat, then – but from whom? Or what?

No time for dawdling! K. Sohail, ever intrepid, was on her way.

Into the jungle I thrashed, catching up as best I could in my socks. The path was shoulder-width, so occasionally the monstrosities of the local flora brushed my body – fronds, spines, thickets, leafy clusters, pronged grasses as sharp as blades, withered tendrils dangling like serpentine hair from the verdant canopy above. And those were just the plants – never mind the menagerie of 'crawling creeps' that surely lurked within.

At any moment some antenna'd vermin might come chirruping out of the underbrush, launch itself with a thrum of whirring wings, latch upon my neck with its barbed feet, winnow into one of my earholes, scurry through the labyrinthine canals therein – trailing corrosive juice – and arrive, triumphantly, to roost and feast upon my brain. As I came crashing up behind K. Sohail, something potentially insectile caressed my inner thigh, sending me into paroxysms of shrieking and a panicked, high-kneed dance. K. Sohail glanced briefly over her shoulder, shook her head, sighed audibly, and forged ahead up that narrow path.

I was amazed: oblivious or indifferent to all the horrors that surrounded us, she retreated, per the sign's instruction, unperturbed. So reckless! Did my companion not hear, amid the underbrush to the right, a millipede's demonic scuttle as it cunningly tracked us, mandibles dripping venom, awaiting an opportune moment to strike? Did she not fear its podiatrically gratuitous gait, its pincered sting? Never mind the birds, warbling all around in a great, shrill chorus of mockery and disdain.

Yet perhaps K. Sohail simply didn't care.

My god. Utter lunacy. What sort of brash madwoman was shepherding us on this 'retreat'? From a few paces behind I watched her, mottled in the rash of sunlight permitted by the jungle canopy, blithely kick aside a clot of brush – were those vipers slithering away into the shadows? (No: twigs.) Yet my fearless leader didn't even break stride.

Though perhaps I was the one being brash?

She, after all, was a professional at security.

What I was witnessing wasn't brazen ignorance, but audacity. A show of nerve! Fearsome mettle! Pluck and valour!

I squinted, reappraising K. Sohail's unfettered march through the trees. I was struck then by the sure-footed, beige thrust of her body through space, the wherewithal and confidence of her steady, propulsive gait. Yes: this was no heedless fool, but a character of great moxie and poise. What a spirit! Like a kind of god, or at least someone who, boldly, believed in something – who might even *believe in herself*. (Unlike I, so ontologically dubious.) Here was a real hero to whom even the treacheries of an island jungle were something to be thwarted and bested, not feared.

With this shift in perception I wondered if I might glean from her some courage of my own. I tried to alter my timid, sock-hopping mince to match her daring tromp along the path. Hopeless – two steps in, a nearby fern wispily stroked my ankle and I launched three feet into the air, whinnying like a pinched mule. This time K. Sohail, plunging ahead into the jungle, didn't so much as glance my way.

Racing to catch up I again admired her resolve: the sturdy thump of her footsteps, chin held high, nary a balk nor panicked yelp, even when the jungle infringed grotesquely upon her person. I was witnessing, I realized, the 'tools for trading' of the professional security guard. And how striking she looked in beige!

Ack – what lechery. Gross. I couldn't very well chase my dignified companion around like some tent-panted pervert.

As I was formulating an apology, K. Sohail stopped, as they say, 'dead on the tracks.' Two great palms drooped over her like palms – of hands, that is – ready to snatch her head from her shoulders and bat it about like a shuttlecock. She remained motionless, staring ahead. I tensed, frozen too, anticipating the signal to re-retreat: back through the hideous, seething jungle, to the beach, to the sea – into its waves and our watery graves.

Instead she beckoned me.

I crept forward, dreading whatever new horror awaited – a pit of snakes, a pit of teeth. But we'd only reached a clearing. The path ended and the jungle opened upon an encampment of sorts: a dozen bamboo huts with grassy roofs over which lorded a hilltop building in steel and reflective glass. This I can only describe as a Welcome Centre, per the banner over its front doors proclaiming WELCOME in a hysterical font, and its central location amid the camp.

– Ah, said K. Sohail sagely.

– Ah? said I, less so.

– The Retreat.

I squinted. And understood: the sign had directed us *to this Retreat*, as in a spot for holidaying – a resort, etc. – and not *in retreat* from anything. I felt relieved, for a moment, before noticing movement in the doors of the Welcome Centre. We'd been spotted. Someone was coming our way.

Remarkably K. Sohail didn't flee. In fact she stepped forward, out of the undergrowth, to greet whoever approached – to greet us in turn? Or to gun us down like cows on the lam?

I watched the figure wind its way down a path from the Welcome Centre and through the huts. What was this? Not a person at all, but something like … a rubbish bin? Or a postbox? It glided as if on wheels or skates.

And then it was upon us.

A column of shiny black plastic about as tall as my chin.

A lime-coloured stripe illuminated its top – or lid. And the lights bent into a smile. And then reorganized into the word *Welcome*.

– WELCOME. YOU MUST BE THE DHALIWALS, spoke the column. Its voice was slightly nasal, but no less human than my own (which I have been told sounds like a duck being beaten to death with another, deader duck). And then it signed off: REGARDS, JEROME.

– The whom? I began, but K. Sohail stomped my socked toes and exploited my cry of agony to captain the conversation:

– Mrs. and Mr. Dhaliwal, certainly, yes.

The column's green lights smiled again, then formed a crude thumbs-up. – GRAND, it said. JEROME WAS WORRED THAT YOU WEREN'T GOING TO MAKE IT. JEROME HEARD OF A HELICOPTER CRASH AT SEA. JEROME ASSUMED IT WAS YOUR TRANSPORT –

– No, interrupted K. Sohail. We are here, and fine.

The column's lights formed an ellipsis that rippled to its end point, again and again. A slight whirring sounded from within its body. It was, I realized, thinking, or computing – or struggling with my companion's nametag, which clearly read: *K. Sohail*.

– JEROME HAS A *DR.* AND MR. DHALIWAL REGISTERED FOR THE TEN DAY 'LOVE INTENSIFIER REBOOT,' said the column finally. REGARDS, JEROME.

– Yes, *Doctor*, of course, said K. Sohail. That is I, Dr. Dhaliwal. And this is my husband, she said, nudging me: Mr. Dhaliwal.

– At your service, I said.

– JEROME IS GLAD TO MEET YOU, said the column, DR. AND MR. DHALIWAL. REGARDS, JEROME.

– Who, may I ask, I asked, is Jerome?

– JEROME IS TO WHOM YOU ARE SPEAKING, said the column. JEROME'S NAME IS JEROME. YOU MAY CALL JEROME JEROME. REGARDS, JEROME.

– You … are Jerome? I ventured.

– JEROME, confirmed Jerome. REGARDS, JEROME.

– Jerome, said K. Sohail.

We stood there for a moment, under the blazing island sun, the three of us – man, woman, and sentient column – digesting this information.

– YOU HAVE NO LUGGAGE? inquired Jerome, its lights forming a question mark. REGARDS, JEROME.

– No, said K. Sohail hastily. We thought it would … Be better … If …

– JEROME CAN PROVIDE THE BASICS OF TOILETRIES, ETCETERA. AND OF COURSE, AS YOU KNOW, THE ONLY CLOTHING PERMITTED HERE AT THE RETREAT IS ROBES, WHICH I WILL PROVIDE SHORTLY. REGARDS, JEROME.

– Robes, I said, will be delightful.

– GOOD, said Jerome. NOW, PLEASE. YOUR WRISTBANDS. REGARDS, JEROME.

A sort of shelf slid out of Jerome's midsection. Upon it sat two orange wristbands outfitted with bar codes. We laid our hands, palms up, atop them, and the things came slithering to life, wrapped our wrists, and snapped closed. The ring of plastic seemed to hum, as if with a current, and its fastener pinched my arm-hair in an excruciating way.

– EXCELLENT. NOW, PLEASE, FOLLOW ME. YOU ARE LATE FOR YOUR INITIAL SESSION. AFTER WHICH I WILL TAKE YOU TO LUNCH. REGARDS, JEROME.

– Session? K. Sohail inquired.

– Lunch? said I.

– OF COURSE. YOUR INTAKE SESSION WITH PROFESSOR SAYER. REGARDS, JEROME.

– And then we get to eat? I asked, my stomach fairly leaping up my throat, out of my mouth, and clambering off to wherever said meal might be on offer.

—YOU ARE REGISTERED FOR PREMIUM ALL-INCLUSIVE: MEALS, DRINKS, SESSIONS, TREATMENT, SPEAKERS, EVENTS, EXCURSIONS, AND ROBES. REGARDS, JEROME.

I exchanged a look with K. Sohail – or, that is, my lovely, very hungry wife, Dr. Dhaliwal. She nodded: a Session, whatever that entailed, would be rewarded with lunch. With a wordless, panicked arch of my eyebrows, I tried to convey the following message:

Are we really going to try to 'pull one very fast' on this officious robot, Jerome, and pretend to be a married couple, one of whom is presumably either a physician or an academic of advanced standing, and at the very least a luminary or expert conferred an honorary doctorate in some professional field or other, perhaps even one that might require said expertise to be tried, questioned, or even put into practice at some point here, on this island – what if our dearly departed Dr. Dhaliwal had been invited to this Retreat, for example, to perform some sort of lecture? Or sit on a panel? Or hypnotize a crowd of rapturous onlookers into believing that they were poultry and cast them clucking about the grounds? Or, even more worryingly, what if the real Dr. Dhaliwal is, or was, a surgeon, who, in the event of some medical emergency here at the Retreat, per its location in 'darkness's heart' (i.e., this jungly island hellscape), would be expected to perform, say, the surgical rescue of a child swallowed by a python – slashing, that is, said python open expertly with a blade, carving the child out from the digestive cavity, resuscitating it, and perhaps even rebuilding the poor little love's mush of a skeleton as a result of the python's bone-crushing constrictions? Are you, K. Sohail, in playing the role, or impersonating, or stealing the identity of the late Dr. Dhaliwal, prepared to embark on a ruse of such mind-boggling complexity and potential peril? Consider the depth of subterfuge and deceit required to maintain our falsified identities, even if the real Dr. and Mr. Dhaliwal are tragically dead at the bottom of the ocean – a tragedy that, keep in mind, we dispassionately witnessed, which makes us not only complicit in the death of the Dhaliwals, but beneficiaries of their demise, having assumed their places at this Retreat. Or worse still, imagine if they have survived said crash and are at this very moment swimming ashore to unmask us as imposters? And what of Mr. Dhaliwal? We have no idea who he is at all. Not even a professional qualification. The fellow could be a hero or a knave, fluent in seventeen languages or a mercury-addled maniac prone to howling like a banshee at the sight of a peeled potato. What role am I meant to play? Who am I now?!

After an unblinking moment, our gazes locked upon each other's, I tilted my eyebrows into a more inquisitive and buoyant position, suggesting:

Though, really, who could have survived a crash like that? Realistically, the real Dhaliwals are fish food. Since we were surely the last people on earth to see them alive, what better way to honour the couple's memory than to assume their places here and behave in an exemplary fashion as testament and commemoration. If imitation is the sincerest form of flattery, shameless impersonation will be a veritable paean to those intrepid lost souls, Dr. and Mr. Dhaliwal, Rest in Peace.

My wife, as it were, shrugged.

Jerome was waiting. The lights on the top of his head formed that repeating ellipsis, like a caterpillar crawling across his head:

– ... ...

– PLEASE, he said eventually. COME WITH JEROME. PROFESSOR SAYER AWAITS. REGARDS, JEROME.

With a final, grim nod, together Dr. Dhaliwal and I headed up the path, following that column of talking plastic to wherever, and whoever, we were supposed to be.

Session #1 Transcript

– Hello, welcome, Dr. and Mr. Dhaliwal, and, if I may, first, please, scan your wristbands, just a slight jolt, a little buzz, nothing to recoil at, there we are, in you come, and, yes, as I was saying, welcome, to this Intake Session, the first of your Daily Sessions, which, as you know, begin now, and, if you wish, may I invite you to sit, and, my apologies, also, just so you are aware, I should inform you, before we go any further, as you can, perhaps, see from the device, there, upon that table, with the red light, that these Sessions are being recorded, albeit, of course, for my own purposes, confidentially, provided neither of you mind, that is, being recorded, by which I mean, of course, during this Intake Session, as well as henceforth, hereafter, in our subsequent Sessions, to document, on tape, not simply for posterity, but for my own revision, and analysis, your Treatment, so that it might, I hope, proceed as successfully, for all of us, myself included, but, primarily, for you, Dr. and Mr. Dhaliwal, as it can.

  – And where should we sit, Professor Sayer?

  – Please, wherever, Mr. Dhaliwal, together, or, certainly, Dr. Dhaliwal, separately, if you prefer, it's why I offer many seating options, as you can see, from the loveseat, armchairs, chaise, and beanbag, as I like to afford my clients a sense of agency, so, please, make yourselves comfortable, however you'd like, and when you're seated, we'll begin.

  – Is where we sit a test?

  – No, no, no tests, Mr. Dhaliwal, not here, which, this space, that is, is intended to promote dialogue, conversation, sincerity, introspection, but, no, where you sit is not a test, nor is any part of our Sessions evaluative, or adjudicated, per se, so, please, sit wherever you'd like, the most important thing being, of course, your comfort, such that this intake session, and all of our Sessions, might proceed as fluidly as possible.

– Why don't I just squeeze in with you, then, Dr. Dhaliwal, my darling? Yes? Fine?

– Fine.

– And, before we begin, if I may, are either of you, and I should have offered this sooner, in need of, and I apologize for not being able to offer coffee or tea, though I find stimulants, how best to say it, cloud the eros, so, then, to drink I can offer only our planet's most superior natural hydrant and lubricant, by which I mean, of course, water, so would either of you, Dr. or Mr. Dhaliwal, or both, like a glass of water?

– My god, I'll take one of those … Ah! How refreshing. Despite being so tepid.

– Doctor, if I may, also, offer you, if you'd like, some water?

– Yes, fine.

– Good, yes, good, please, drink, good, and would you, Mr. Dhaliwal, like, as they say, a refill, and, Doctor, would you, also, like a refill?

– My god, please!

– I'm fine.

– Fine, yes, good, shall we begin, then, by you, by which, my apologies, I mean both of you, Dr. and Mr. Dhaliwal, telling me, or explaining, why you are here, together?

– Together?

– I think the good doctor – my sweet, beautiful wife – is wondering if you mean together, here, at the Retreat? Or together … as a couple?

– Well perhaps, if I may, Mr. Dhaliwal, it might be an idea, at least, to begin, in this intake session, for the benefit of the therapeutic process, and so that I might learn something of you both, that you speak only of yourself, individually, although, of course, from that, per my professional training, I will understand you collectively as well, that is, your relationship, so, yes, might we now proceed, forward, with your Treatment?

– We met at a mall.

– Dr. Dhaliwal was working there. As the mall's … doctor. And I was …

– He was working there also.

– Yes, making work. And living there also.

– Living, that is, in a mall?

– Yes?

– Intriguing …

– One might say that.

– Oh, I think, yes, Dr. Dhaliwal, to say the least, yes, one might find such a story of romantic, and eventual marital, genesis, or origination, most intriguing, though please, I say this without judgment, I am only voicing my intrigue at your, as in *you*, Mr. Dhaliwal, but also both of you, collectively, at the intrigue, I think, of your particular living arrangements, that is, which instigated your meeting, and dare I venture, your union.

– Our *union*?

– Yes, Dr. Dhaliwal, no need to recoil, everything here is confidential, there's nothing we can't discuss, including unions matrimonial, or sensual, or other, and, speaking of, I can see, just now, by the way you, Mr. Dhaliwal, have seized, and now clutch, your wife's hand, that is, with your own, trembling, moist hand, such that I can, unimpeachably, as a couples' therapist, attest, I know a passionate union when I see one, and as such, I am certain, professionally, that you two are, very much, I think, in love.

– Clutch?

– And yet, not to second-guess you, but, as we know, you have come here, to the Retreat, to work on, if not your relationship, then at least some aspect of it, to which I say bravo, of course, as a professional, but also, as you can imagine, a human being, who also, please forgive me, admires, between two people, any union of the soul, as well as, let's not forget, once again, the union of the corpus, as we must, I believe, celebrate, as it were, freely, the pleasures of the flesh, and despite my professional perspective I am, as I've mentioned, only a human being, who hungers, in fact, for those very same pleasures, and as such I appreciate, very much, as I observe you closely now, the way in which your thighs, for example, Dr. and Mr. Dhaliwal, are touching, ever so softly, just pressing against each other, almost tantalizingly, so the flesh, so supple, begins to tingle with anticipation for more, for greater and more exploratory touch.

– Sorry?

– And, as you'll discover, in your room, your *private* room, that is, with multiple locks on the door, to ensure said privacy, such that you might, dare I suggest, undertake whatever mutually agreeable activities, that is, to express the poetics of your eroticism, together, and should you need prompting, you'll find some helpful instructional videos available in your in-hut entertainment service, which, perhaps, you might follow, tonight, and perhaps beyond, such that these videos might guide the Intimate Sessions you enjoy, here, this week, to the letter, per the checklist you'll find, helpfully provided, in your hut, whereupon you can, I advise, for our purposes here, as well as for my edification and consultation, document your, shall we say, escapades, and from which I might, per my professional acumen, evaluate your performance, per the video model provided to you.

– You want us to copy the videos?

– Pardon me, Professor Sayer, but like my wife, I'm rather confused: we're to copy the videos and then … file a report? To see how well we've done?

– Indeed, splendid, you have it, blessed Dhaliwals, I'm so pleased, you've grasped the key concepts, but yes, a mall, was it, you said, Dr. Dhaliwal, where you met?

– A mall, yes. Where we met.

– And where, my darling, we first fell in love!

Two

Robes flapping, we stumbled out of our inaugural Treatment with the penetrating, progressively stimulated Professor Sayer feeling spent – emotionally, intellectually, physically, existentially, logistically and, due to the Professor's succubal prompting, erogenously. My 'wife,' per her deadpan manner, maintained the ruse without breaking a sweat, but never have my loins – and heart! – sustained such relentless clenching.

For an hour, with nothing to sustain us but water, we had pretended to be Dr. and Mr. Dhaliwal, and the fiction of our subterfuge had somehow merged with the reality of our shared history. Our versions of the Dhaliwals were extravagant millionaires capable of chartering a private helicopter to an all-inclusive Retreat, yet we had also somehow met while working/living in a mall. We were lifelong lovers who, even when urged to fondle each other freely (in order for the Professor to observe and, per her professional expertise, better comprehend our relationship) could only manage the most chaste intimacies: a hand squeezed, a knee patted, a loving kick to the shin. We claimed shyness, jetlag, morning breath, and my wife's propensity to, when stimulated, ravish me to such orgasmic oblivion that it would derail any attempt at therapy. Surely such performances were better saved for our second Session, no? *Yes*, we demurred.

So K. Sohail – or, rather, my wife, the respected Dr. Dhaliwal – and I, Mr. Dhaliwal, exited this first Session in need of private consultation to 'straighten our stories.' The improvisations we had produced and attempted to harmonize in real time had revealed our ruse as a flimsy, amorphous thing. What did our therapist, and the organizers of the Retreat, know about the actual Dhaliwals? How far had we strayed from the truth? We'd assumed they were 'our age,' as I assumed K. Sohail was mine – which, surely, she was. But what if they weren't? Was the Professor, as we blundered around the carpeted maze of the Welcome Centre, making calls to management or the authorities, alerting them to the presence of two interlopers, and perhaps even summoning a marine unit to dredge the depths of the seas for a downed chopper and the real Dhaliwals' waterlogged remains?

But wait, I thought. Perhaps it was possible that our mistruths might be construed as diversionary tactics: perhaps, I hoped, the good Professor cross-referenced our answers to the facts on file and diagnosed us not as imposters but a couple in deep crisis who, under examination, resorted to fabrications rather than confront the harrowing reality of their (failing?) marriage. Perhaps the Professor would even regard us, the Dhaliwals, as a quandary, a 'toughened nut to crack open' with the sledgehammer of psychoanalysis, and that our obfuscations, inventions, and outright lies weren't fraudulent but symptomatic of profound emotional, romantic, and personal wounds. Perhaps, I thought with lifting spirits, we even presented a welcome, invigorating challenge to Professor Sayer and her curiously erotic approach to the talk-therapy process.

I realized that my wife, Dr. Dhaliwal, had stopped to gaze out a second-floor window over the Retreat: the scattering of cabins, the jungle, the bluish haze of the ocean, and the cerulean sky, which the sun seemed to hold aloft like a thumbtack made of light.

– I thought that went well? I ventured.

The good doctor merely continued to catalogue the grounds, her gaze sweeping from one side to the other – as a prisoner might, seeking escape? Or with the itinerating ambitions of a conqueror? I did not know my wife well enough to say.

And then a nasal voice chimed at my elbow, startling me enough that my bladder loosened two almost unnoticeable droplets into my robes.

– JEROME TRUSTS THAT YOUR INTAKE SESSION WAS A SUCCESS? REGARDS, JEROME.

– A veritable triumph, I enthused.

– AND NOW LUNCH? REGARDS, JEROME.

– Yes, said Dr. Dhaliwal. Please, Jerome: some lunch.

Our robotic guide zipped off down the corridor, and with us following behind narrated the Retreat's various features and facilities as we passed them. These included:

A Games Room, from which resounded the zaps and bloops of arcade consoles and digital slot machines; the clack and scutter of billiard balls; the tick-tock of ping-pong; the whizz and thunk of darts hurled at a board of cork, then plucked free with a greasy slurp; the lugubrious clack of checkers hopped around a gameboard and mounted one upon the next in the triumphant manoeuvre known as 'crowning'; the more subtle, velvety shush of chess pieces slid around their own, identical yet infinitely more sophisticated gameboard, and the slight gasp of an incredulous knave or clergyman vanquished by a lowly pawn; the delirious jangle of a pinball machine; the whirr and clatter of the roulette wheel; the skeletal rattle of dice; cries of victory; cries of defeat; a sole, plaintive voice imploring Lady Luck and Sir Serendipity both: *Fortune be mine, today!*

Then: a Fitness and Beauty Realm, from which wafted odours of chlorine; the wetly aged cheddar of sweat-sodden gym mats; the soporific caress of eucalyptus; the musty fug of the steam bath; the tangy cocktail of steel, rubber, and testosterone that belies a weight room's parade of hubris and puffery; a sauna's woodsy conflagration; soap; commercial deodorizers masking poorly the pheromonal stink of hand-kneaded human flesh; chemical masks, washes, rinses, and scrubs; the pong of feet and their attendant fungi; cucumber; mint; a bowl of cherries; an ice machine; urine; blood; vomit; hope.

Next: a pub-cum-night club called, simply, BAR. Behind its eponymous bar, festooned with upturned stools, a backlit shelving unit showcased every liquor of the rainbow, each bottle glowing radioactively. To the left of the bar a checkered, electrified dance floor, which a disco-jig could ignite into a frenzy of light, was overseen by a glittering ball (its twirling chaos dormant for now), and two human-sized birdcages on raised daises; to the bar's right several low tables were scattered in the gloom. As I swept past I imagined the clammy debauchery, lecherous fondling, and frantic ululations of a classic 'night upon the town' here in this cave-like hovel, the various nectars of the devil slurped in the dark.

Beyond that, heralded by a cinema's epileptic marquee, was an Arts & Entertainment Hub, through the open doors of which, as we hurried past, I glimpsed a stage bordered by red velvet curtains slightly parted (like the lips of a seductive couples therapist); the graveyard of an empty orchestra pit, with music stands for headstones, plus a gong; a glass-doored shower; a roped-off ring – for unarmed combat? – and, from which to observe whatever transpired on-stage, a great sweep of amphitheatrical seating from floor to ceiling, each chair as plush as a fluffed-up cockatoo.

And, finally, after several bewildering twists and turns that took us alongside great floor-to-ceiling vitrines overlooking the island and sea, into interior hallways with views of nothing but wall, seemingly back past Professor Sayer's office to a library, then down a sloping passageway and through a doorway draped with plastic slats, veering around two sharp corners and three doglegs, into a cramped, concrete area I can only describe as 'the mainframe' (a gauntlet of towering computers, all knobs and wires and circuitry, which emitted a low growl matched only by the more peptic and the despairing growl of our indigent appetites), then up an escalator to a landing, to a mezzanine, to an antechamber, to a vestibule, to an atrium, before at last we pushed through a set of French doors that flapped and gaped like our own ravenous, salivating jaws, into, at last, the Dining Hall, where Jerome would provide us with lunch.

Or I should say: where lunch would be provided as if gifted from the heavens. My god, what a bounty! Even though we were latecomers, and clearly the rest of the inhabitants, or holiday-goers, or Retreaters of the Retreat had already supped from the proverbial and in certain instances literal trough of the Dining Hall, I couldn't believe the range – and excess – of cuisines on offer.

First, Jerome had us scan our wristbands at a turnstile just inside the entrance. When these permitted us through, we were outfitted with plates the size and girth of manhole covers; I needed both hands to hold mine upright. Then our robot host instructed us to brave the gauntlet of food tables of the Dining Hall, loading our plates as we went, until we graduated to a seating area at the back, where we might enjoy our bounties.

– All one can eat? I asked.

– MORE SO EVEN. IT'S ENCOURAGED. REGARDS, JEROME.

So Dr. Dhaliwal and I left him behind and began. We entered the buffet with the tentative shuffle of anyone humbled and overwhelmed by choice, despite our bellies convulsing with a hunger so violent it had become a kind of intestinal grief.

The first table presented an elaborate display of seafood, featuring a veritable aquarium's worth of marine life splayed upon ice and arranged artfully, with either gentle irony or heartlessness, into the shape of a trawler: salmon formed the hull and marlin the gunwales; the deck was crabmeat mashed to a paste and reconstituted as planks; the masts were stacked rings of calamari; the sails were sculpted sheets of, I think, porpoise-hide, and the masthead was a single rouge-roasted lobster, which vomited a steady torrent of liquified butter that threatened to capsize the 'ship,' decadently.

– No thanks, said my wife, Dr. Dhaliwal. I can't even think about eating fish.

– Me neither, said her husband, I.

So on we moved to the fruit table, upon which we glimpsed melons halved and spattered with a limpid goo of liquified lychee; apples cored and whittled into lily-like shapes, with a single seed crowning the parted lips of gleaming flesh; a blueberry impregnating the gaping orifice of every raspberry; mangoes and papayas skinned and sculpted into a pulpy orgy, oozing and moist; lemons, limes, kumquats, grapefruits and pomelos sliced and assembled into a variegated spectacle of citric miscegenation; a banana driving up between the humped, shaggy mounds of two coconuts, its skin peeled back and a pearl of juice glistening at the tip of the creamy glans within.

– Let's keep going, suggested Dr. Dhaliwal.

Then came the meats: great hunks of the stuff cleaved expertly from the bone by some master butcher or chef and then pulverized, salted, spiced, plugged into a sleeve of the creature's own innards, hung to desiccate, and finally sliced into flaps and layered like shingles in a greasy, roseate display. Beside this were the raw cuts, every steak and shank and hock threaded with pale fat and swimming in pools of its own bloody runoff, so fresh nary a maggot could be seen for miles. Amid this menagerie of mammalian flesh raged a fire where, shockingly, one was expected to flame-cook one's own supper! I pictured myself charring a tender morsel to blackened waste … No thanks; culinary enterprise was best left to the experts.

So on we shuffled to the Veggie Cart, a wagon with its twin handles propped on barrels – very rustic, very pastoral, as if asses had heaved the thing here straight from the farm. Yet all I could see was bush: too much greenery, too leafy, as if the jungle had come seeping out of the treeline to tempt our appetites; I imagined it later, cuddled up in our guts, rousing its demonic tendrils to strangle us from within.

I urged my wife onward, shuddering and not looking back.

The next display was the Carb Bar. This was heralded by a container of breadsticks around which someone had spilled heaps of loose grains (oats, barley, wheat, various chaffs and shafts and thistly stalks), though it was unclear if these were decorative, on offer for raw consumption, or flagrantly wasteful. Displayed in glass jars were rices brown and white, wild and tame, all begging for a good steaming. Then the loaves – honeyed and cheesed, flecked with seeds, crusty, gouged into bowls and incestuously filled with croutons – and the pastas, bowtie and beyond, including flat, jaundiced sheets like blank papyrus awaiting the wisdom of the ancients. Oh, and there were potatoes too, in all the colours of a brown, boring rainbow, from beige to chestnut, available for boiling, roasting, toasting, home-frying, mashing, smashing or, even, to the most daring chef, scalloping – like a doily.

– Not in the mood for starch, said Dr. Dhaliwal.

– Nor I, I concurred.

The cheeses followed, in wedges and slices and rounds, waxed and creamed, the whole table seeming to shimmer behind a malodorous wall of fungal nether regions, bad meat ripening in the mid-July sun, sleet-wet sled-dogs bedding down in the igloo, guano, bog-men rising from thousand-year graves with their eyes weeping pus in goopy threads and their flesh crumbling like the centuries-ravaged pages of some cryptic codex, the eleventh week of a garbage-retrieval strike, a hospital sickbay during 'puke season,' the socks of rainforest activists, and also just the faintest hint of rosemary.

– Pass, said Dr. Dhaliwal.

I acquiesced.

On we went, arriving at an entire display dedicated to mayonnaise-based salads, including tuna, salmon, pasta, Waldorf, egg, potato, apple 'n' celery, shredded carrot 'n' raisin 'n' nut, three-bean, four-pulse, and a number of velvety concoctions that evaded taxonomy. The table also offered 'curried' versions of these same salads – which, I assumed, involved nothing more than a dash or two of some powdered spice mix in a kind of pandering ethnic panic.

More wearied than repulsed, my wife and I swept onward with our plates – past sandwiches sawn into triangles and stacked like sandbags to ward off enemy invasions, past the red-light district of the 'Pizza Studio,' where four rubbery pies twirled listlessly under garish heat-lamps, and past something called the 'Noodle Spot,' which featured several bowls of squiggly heaps and an electric wok; presumably one chucked one's own noodles into the pan and nudged them around until they were warm enough to stomach.

We arrived, ultimately, at a dessert station, where amid sundry cakes and cookies and tarts and tortes, a machine threatened to spiral pastel-coloured soft-serve into wax-paper cups. The toppings were legion: sprinkles; nuts; florid shards of candy; flakes, chunks, bits, and nibs of chocolate inescapably reminiscent of rabbit droppings; nougat, and so on. But we could hardly think of dessert when this was a *desert* island; and besides, we'd not even selected a shred of our 'main' to warrant some sweet, celebratory finale.

And so we emerged from the smorgasbord with empty plates.

Jerome wheeled up and paused before us, the ellipsis dancing across his head.

– JEROME IS CONFUSED, he said. YOU'VE CHOSEN … NOTHING? REGARDS, JEROME.

My wife and I gazed back over that scenic and copious and exhausting assortment of foods miscellaneous and fine. None of it appealed. Why? What was wrong with us? We hung our heads. We were still so hungry. And yet Jerome was right: we'd failed to 'eat all we could eat;' we'd not managed to eat at all.

– Is there anything else? I tried to sound hopeful.

– … … …, said Jerome's head.

We waited.

– …

And waited.

– …

Dr. Dhaliwal coughed.

– …, said Jerome's head.

Finally, with a faint sigh, Jerome glided to one side, revealing, pressed up in the far corner of the room, a wobbly-legged card table. It bore no munificent cornucopia, no artful harvest: only a greasy brown mound and a cylinder of brown drink.

– Is it? I wondered aloud. *Could it be?*

We hurried over. Upon a plastic tray sat a single, picked-over, near skeletal carcass of a spit-roasted chicken, and a plastic pitcher of cloudy tea that was neither hot nor iced, but some ambivalent temperature in between.

– Chicken, said Dr. Dhaliwal.

– And tea, addended I.

To Jerome's dismay we conveyed the tray to the nearest dining table (white cloth, upturned wine glasses, spirals of butter in a bone china dish), and set upon it with our hands, washing down each gristly bite with bitter, tepid gulps straight from the jug.

Chicken and tea – it was what we deserved.

It was who we were.

After lunch Jerome required us to join the rest of the Retreaters for the 'Afternoon Speakers Series,' already underway. Speedily we were guided through the labyrinth of corridors down into the basement. A dingily carpeted hallway led us to the Conference Room, from which came the unmistakable bell-like sound of a Speaker – that is, the electronic device that employs magnetic and acoustic wizardry to augment sound, but also the sort of person who speaks, professionally, to seekers of guidance and hope.

A placard beside the door introduced this Speaker as Mr. Brad Beard.

The good doctor and I scanned our wristbands, flinched at the mild electrocution, slipped inside the doors, and stationed ourselves with admirable decorum at the back of the darkened room. Above the bulbous shadows of two dozen seated human figures, we had a decent view of the stage and the man grandstanding upon it.

Brad Beard was well-named: exuberantly bearded, spotlit, robes flowing. On his face he wore mirrored sunglasses, a headset microphone, and an expression of contemplation: fingers tented under his chin, squinting and frowning slightly. My god, had he been waiting for us? I feared we'd interrupted the proceedings, or, worse, delayed them, and Brad Beard was about to have his way with us, orally. But before I could suggest that we flee, Jerome closed the door behind us.

– No, Brad Beard roared, that's not what True Unity is.

Ah, we'd only entered to a dramatic pause. Rebuke averted!

But rather than edifying us about the true nature of True Unity, the Speaker lapsed again into silence. He squinted, pursed his lips, shook his head: gestures of appraisal, of the mystic assessing his disciples' merit. The whole room held its collective breath: Were we worthy? Were we good?

Finally, grudgingly, Beard lifted his hands, fingers intertwined.

– You see?

Applause resounded around the room. I clapped along, trusting that this pantomime offered great wisdom and I need only keep up. (My wife, meanwhile, crossed her arms.)

– You see? Just there, like that? If I pull one side, the other side holds. And look here: I pull on the *other* side? It … holds … too.

– He's right! corroborated some zealot at the front.

Brad released his hands to point at whomever had spoken, wagging his finger – in solidarity, but also admonishment.

– See this chubby guy here, he's trying to get it. He wants to understand. He's at least got some idea of what it means to reach Peak Cohesion. But let's not get ahead of ourselves. There's no way you're there just yet, Porkpie.

Laughter stuttered through the room.

– Nope. Not by a longshot. And I'm sorry, but just from looking at you I can tell that you've got a long uphill climb ahead and carrying all that weight's going to be a real battle. But anyway – is this your husband right here? The portly fellow with the close-set eyes? Why don't you two stand up?

The zealot and another man rose, turned, waved shyly to the rest of the group. To my surprise, neither was remotely 'chubby' nor 'portly,' but a statuesque paragon of the male form, with taut and chiselled musculature bulging each set of robes. Yet no one returned their wave, afraid of being implicated in whatever humiliation was afoot.

– Look at these two adorable fatsos, said Beard. Aren't they made for each other?

A few noncommittal grunts could have meant yes, or no, depending what Brad Beard wanted to elicit; his agenda was unclear and terrifying.

– How long have you corpulent gentlemen been married?

The fellows' voices were feeble, but I thought I heard something like 'ten years,' or 'we're not,' or 'please leave us alone.'

– Fine, fine, said Brad Beard. But I wonder: have the two of you ever, in your entire gluttonous, butter-swilling time together, *really* experienced True Unity? And I mean a Peak Cohesion of True Unity so true and unified it's not even two words anymore.

He paused. I sensed everyone in the room, myself included and Dr. Dhaliwal excepted, leaning, like weeds to the rain, for the nourishment of what might follow.

– I call that, friends?

Another pause.

– I call that … Trunity.

More gasps. Hoots, hollers. A yodel. High-fives matrimonial and extramarital. Dr. Dhaliwal glared at my upraised hand. So I just pumped my fist and cried, – Huzzah!

– Yup. Trunity, let me tell you … But what are your names, gentlemen?

Something was said. The Speaker shook his head, displeased.

– No, that's no good. I can't pronounce those. Let's just call you Tubs and Pudding.

He pivoted away to address the rest of the room, turning the couple into a sideshow.

– You see Tubs and Pudding here, they're not happy.

Someone booed.

– Easy now, it's not their fault. I was the same as them, once, long ago: ignorant, hopeless, scantily bearded, hopelessly overweight. Back then I thought True Unity was two words. I really thought that, can you imagine? I had no idea that what I should have been seeking was something way more true, way more unified.

He grinned at the 'amen's rippling around the room.

– Trunity is about Truth, check. It's also about Unity: check. But it's not about Truth *and* Unity, if that makes sense. You need to stop thinking about True Unity as truth paired with unification. You need to start thinking, friends – and no, Tubs and Pudding, don't you dare sit down – about Trunity as a single entreaty. Look at these two. These poor, confused, hopelessly obese men. Tackling life like one big hot fudge sundae. Waddling around their crummy apartment, searching, always searching. For what? Cheese? Mints? A couch-buried crust from some long-lost sub? People, is that what life's about? Is that what *marriage* is about?

– No! chorused the crowd, I enthusiastically among them.

Dr. Dhaliwal sighed.

– No, chuckled Brad Beard. No, you're goddamn right it's not. That's not Trunity. Trunity is a state of being. It's remembering what hasn't happened yet. It's love turned inside out. It's a oneness with all things living, dead, and other. It's breathing – Brad Beard flapped his hands as gills and formed a puckery fish-face with his lips – every breath not just like it's your last, but it's *everyone's* last. When you're practicing Trunity – I mean really *practicing* it, holistically – you become your own shadow. You're a cool dance in the night. You're sailing into the great beyond. Your nerves are zinging, your soul is singing, and touching yourself should feel like setting your own flesh on fire.

– Exactly, that is, *yes!* cried Professor Sayer.

– And when it comes to marriage, continued Brad Beard, deepening his voice to summon even more profound wisdom, two souls can share that Trunity energy pulsing through each of you, which nobody can deny, because your collective magnetism is exactly that: a magnet, and you fuse together, positive and negative, until you're one melded one. That's the goal of goals, the light of lights. People always ask me, *Yeah Brad my man, who's been my hero since the get, but what about Peak Cohesion, I thought that was the point of all this.* First of all: that's the dumbest question I've ever heard. You're asking it like Peak Cohesion is something you can attain on your own. Ha! How can you cohese with nobody to cohese with? You want Peak Cohesion? You need another. You start with two bodies, then you find Trunity – and then?!

He clapped his hands with the force of a land mine exploding in the room. Everyone leapt! And then we settled, shell-shocked, as he linked fingers again and held his fused hands above his head. (What a showman! Almost literally electrifying!)

– And then, Brad Beard growled, you and your lover pass through to *the other side.*

He released his hands, removed his sunglasses, flung them offstage, returned his hands to cradle the back of his neck, and titled his chin so his gaze turned heavenward.

– And what then? he whispered. What is even on *the other side?*

The question hung in the air. I found myself on my tiptoes, with a ravenous pang juddering through my whole body. But Brad Beard said nothing. Only stared into the rafters, lips pursed as if for a kiss. The silence felt like a cage – or, no, the opposite: more like the universe, expanding infinitely and vacuously, all around.

My god, Beard, you excruciating demon, tell us!

Finally, he chuckled. Shook his head. Dropped his hands to his sides. Shrugged.

– If you want the answer to that little paradoxical, friends? If you really want to discover what's over there? Well you and your beloveds are going to have to stick around to the end of the Retreat, pay close attention, grow your beards, do the private work in your huts and with my esteemed and attentive colleague Rosa G. Sayer, commit to the principles of Trunity I've outlined here today, and find out for your g-darn selves.

– Certainly one of the finest Speakers I've ever seen.

– Brad Beard? Never seen a Speaker like it.

– That Trunity stuff, man … I always thought Truth and Unity were separate things. Totally life-altering to think they were a single entreaty the whole time.

– We usually like to be able to see a Speaker's face, so with the sunglasses *and* the beard it felt like maybe Brad's got something to hide. But if you think of him like a secret agent – like a secret agent of the soul – it totally works. And we came to really dig the shades. Turns out they're offered with the Diamond Ratifier Package so we're going to Tier Up and order like sixty pairs.

– I kind of didn't understand all of it? Especially the Trunity stuff? Is that the same as Peak Cohesion or, like, something else? Super jealous of his beard though.

– My partner and I knew this year's Retreat was going to be special. But it's not even Night One yet and both of us can already feel our Core Principles dynamizing!

– It's Mr. Beard's grasp of rhetoric one finds most impressive. Certainly one admires the insights, the showmanship, the deep wisdom, the scope of his ontology and the sheer power of his oration. But what is truly flabbergasting is the transcendental praxis concealed within Mr. Beard's dialectic. He's a poet of the infinite, a bard of the beyond.

– JEROME IS PLEASED THAT EVERYONE ENJOYED THE AFTERNOON SPEAKERS' SERIES SO THOROUGHLY. REGARDS, JEROME.

– Beard's right, you know: pull one side, the other holds; pull the other, vice-a-versa.

– Going to be hard to look at my husband now, to be honest. A nice enough guy, don't get me wrong. But compared to Brad Beard, it's not even close.

– A very, very good Session. Not great. But very, very good.

– My wife and I have a signed copy of *Conjoining We* framed above our bed at home. Every Wednesday night, when we try to achieve Carnal Fruition, we like to think Brad's cheering us on. Finally seeing him live was amazing, but we're most excited that this week the man himself might be listening in only a few huts away.

– Honestly, not his best Session. He's clearly lost a step since the funicular accident. Still, I'd rather a brain-damaged Brad Beard than that blathering fool we saw at WellFest last year. I mean, *Soul Tissue*? Have you ever heard anything so misguided, so deranged?

– For me and my wife it's consistency. You see Brad Beard on a Symposium Manifest, you know you're getting the real deal. And Actionable Processes you can take straight to the g-darn bank.

– Didn't you think he was a little … mean? My husband and I aren't even fat. And even if we were, why –

– Listen to Tubby and Lardo! They don't know how lucky they are, singled out for Lessoning by none other than Sir Bradley Beard (knightship pending). Guys like these two jellyrolls probably think Trunity's some kind of cucumber sandwich.

– Cucumber *and egg* sandwich!

– Anyway, a great afternoon.

– A truly great afternoon.

– Totally agree. And speaking as a regular at Brad B.'s symposia, I'll add that the last time I saw him with a lover – not you, sugar, one of the other ones – was during his tour for *Loving with Both Hands*. Which everyone agrees was then a high point in his illustrious career. And we were blown away! I remember afterward just sort of wandering the streets in a daze, trying to digest what we'd seen and heard and learned and, you know, lived. But this? This, here, today? Nothing could have prepared any of us for *this*.

Our accommodations were not, as I'd hoped, dormitory-style barracks with mercifully discrete bunks, but instead a windowless bamboo hut anchored by a heart-shaped waterbed, complete with faux-fur headboard and a swing dangling above its satin sheets. On a shelf nearby, an array of dungeon equipment was close at hand.

I also inventoried, more innocuously, a nightstand, wastebasket, and three-drawer dresser – and, affixed to the hut's far wall, a massive high-definition television set the size of a bedsheet.

– YOUR QUARTERS, said Jerome. BATHROOMS ARE IN HUT #7. PLEASE RECALL THAT PROFESSOR SAYER REQUIRES YOU FOR YOUR FIRST OFFICIAL SESSION THIS EVENING. AND NOW: ENJOY. REGARDS, JEROME.

Once he was gone, Dr. Dhaliwal toed the mattress, which jiggled and rippled.

– You can have the bed, she said. I'll sleep on the floor.

At this I felt some relief, but also disappointment. The sensation of clutching my wife (back when she was still K. Sohail) was fading, and I felt my soul grasping after that sensation of communion; sharing a bed might have occasioned more of the same, while also stilling Jerome's suspicions should he come wheeling by in the dead of night to confirm our marital bliss.

An explosion of light and sound interrupted my contemplation.

The TV had come on.

I heard moaning. I saw flesh. Human skin, guttural sounds. I scanned the room but saw no 'remote.' The TV had awakened of its own accord, or perhaps per a timer: here was the instructional video Professor Sayer had inadequately warned us about.

And it was made of pornography.

I gawked at that fleshy, slippery rapture writ large in gaudily tinted pixels. Amid its bricolage of flesh emerged searching hands, curling toes, moistened mouths, gleaming teeth, curling tongues, rapturous glares, oozy goo, a voluptuous buttock, a 'full' bosom – and nether regions shot in intimate, full-frontal close-up, as if they were actors themselves.

The scene ended. Another began: two bodies disrobing – the classic opening gambit of human lust.

– For the love of god, muttered my wife, turn that garbage off.

A chance for heroism! I bounded across our hut. But upon the set I could locate nothing like a power button. In such proximity to the screen, what transpired upon it now implicated me: a shirt came over a head, a leg wiggled out of a pant – and another!

– Pull the plug!

But I detected no cord. Meanwhile that fleshy spectacle writhed away, indomitable and obscene in its corporal revelations – elbows, kneecaps, ankles, earlobes, uvulae, phalanges – zoomed in so close I could fairly smell their salty musk.

And then I noticed, on the wall beside the TV, a clipboard hanging on a nail. Affixed to the clipboard was a checklist. I recalled Sayer's threat that we were meant to 'play along' to the videos; here was the form to log our performance for her approval. I scanned the terms. My god! What salacious contortions would be required for a Burgling Wonder? Or, for that matter, something called the Chocolate Reverse? Never mind the menace of Reheated Gravy, the Plunger, a Snootling Tuesday, Celery Yogurt, Calling All Cars, the Vanishing Egg, It Takes One to Know One, a Sleepy Bruno, a Bruised Larry, a Throttled Jake, an Oily Headlock and, most terrifying of all, Lady's Choice.

A taxonomy of filth! Which, worryingly, hinted at the sorts of carnal gymnastics I was barely capable of alone, never mind under the watchful eye (and hands, and pubis) of my ostensible if unwilling wife. I turned my attention to the TV set and the oozy, licentious festival broadcast upon it. And, despite everything, found myself riveted, and rapt, and watching.

The nosing, the nibbling, the teasing, the suckling, the slurping, the gobbling, the tickling, the rejecting, the apologizing, the consenting, the resuming, the smooching, the fondling, the probing, the groaning, the moaning, the dampening, the blooming, the displaying, the admiring, the kneeling, the splaying, the looming, the welcoming, the mounting, the easing, the grinding, the hastening, the riding, the turning, the thrusting, the thrusting, the thrusting, the thrusting, the thrusting, the thrusting, the thrusting, the thrusting, the hitching, the resting, the breathing, the hydrating, the repositioning, the resuming, the thrusting, the thrusting, the thrusting, the flipping, the thrusting, the heightening, the grunting, the thrusting, the shrieking, the thrusting, the hollering, the thrusting, the imploring, the thrusting, the communing, the approving, the thrusting, the thrusting, the thrusting, the thrusting, the pausing, the seizing, the lingering, the convulsing, the collapsing, the weeping, the nothing, the nothing, the mopping, the disposing, the consoling, the settling, the thinking, the considering, the evaluating, the affirming, the thanking, the snoring, the enquiring, the snoring, the sighing, the staring, the reminiscing, the prospecting, the acquiescing, the fading, the fading, the fading, the sleeping, the dreaming, the end.

Session #2 Transcript

– Hello, Dr. and Mr. Dhaliwal, again, and, to begin, a reminder, which is that this, our second Session, albeit the first Session, actually, of your Treatment, proper, which will proceed, henceforth, recorded, again, for my own purposes, and, might I say, how good to see you again, and, if I may ask, how was your first day, here, at the Retreat?

– Fine.

– My wife is being characteristically taciturn, Professor. We've had a fabulous day! Truly splendid! The lunch buffet, Brad Beard, the instructional videos – we've enjoyed ourselves tremendously, as you'll see from how ably we ticked off your checklist, right down to the Bubbling Gluepot. A tough one, that. But we managed.

– Well, that is wonderful to hear, Mr. Dhaliwal, I am glad, for both of you, although, if I may ask, more specifically, how you've settled in, by which I mean, precisely, are you finding the lodgings adequately comfortable, that is, comfortable enough to feel, as it were, at home, or, further, as comfortable as you might feel in your own bed, that is, such that you feel comfortable to, without prompting, unreservedly and passionately fornicate?

– Ha! Please see the list. Have you ever seen such a robust column of checkmarks?

– Laughter, Mr. Dhaliwal, to my question, is an intriguing response, and as such I must, and please forgive my candour here, demand, what, exactly, you find so amusing, to my inquiry regarding the natural, beautiful and satiating act of fornication, about which, in the context, especially, of a romantic and sexual partnership, there is nothing amusing, or upsetting, unless, that is, you find something amusing, or upsetting, about fornicating with your wife, the objectively attractive Dr. Dhaliwal?

– No, of course not, Professor Sayer. With my objectively attractive wife? Obviously anyone would be lucky to fornicate with her. I was laughing precisely due to how relentlessly we fornicate, per that list. Don't we, Dr. Dhaliwal? It's virtually nonstop! Unreservedly, copiously, exhaustively, fervently – fornicating, always fornicating.

– Indeed.

– Ah, yes, good, Dr. Dhaliwal, good to hear from you, and, yes, as you say, *indeed*, although, if I may, Mr. Dhaliwal, while copiousness and fervency are, without doubt, important elements of fornication, I worry that you have not mentioned passion, because certainly it is passion, isn't it, if you will forgive the analogy, that oils the engine of fornication, in addition, of course, to bodily secretions, which provide more explicitly literal lubrication, and, while I'm thinking of it, the Retreat offers, in our Love Shop, for sale, many creams, lotions, fluids, and other excellent products, synthetic and naturally derived, if you seek supplementary lubrication, that is, for your fornicating needs?

– Oh, we appreciate that, Professor, but we've no trouble in that regard. Wouldn't you agree, my darling? When it comes to our fornicating needs?

– Yes. Fine.

– Ah, excellent, as you wish, and, per your own admissions about the frequency and, was it, fervency of your fornication, if you see my nostrils flaring, now, it's because of my professional capacity to sense pheromonal wavelengths, and, I must admit, I'm not detecting, olfactorily, any of the usual feline, or aquatic, odours, which signify the detritus of recent fornication, and as such I must ask, for the sake of our work, here, in your Treatment, when the last time, specifically, outside of the list – a formality, a kind of training – it was that you fornicated?

– Forty-five minutes ago.

– Yes, on the dot! What a precise memory for fornication she has, my objectively attractive wife. And then we washed together, didn't we, you rapacious demon? Specifically to cleanse us of the catlike and fishy odours of which the Professor speaks.

– Ah, how, I must say, intriguing.

– Come now, Professor. Surely per your professional expertise you recognize in us an excruciatingly normal, obstinately passionate, happily married couple who wile away their days fornicating until the 'cows return'? Look how, even in this moment, I can barely keep my hands off – ow!

– Apologies, Professor. Sometimes I punch him, I'm so passionately aroused.

Three

The daily routine at the Retreat began thusly: breakfast at 7 a.m., then a morning Stretching Circle. These sorts of endeavours, at least in their Westernized incarnations, are ordinarily characterized by almost militaristic uniformity – the leader kinks into a backbend, pelvis saluting the stars, and so, in perfect synchronicity, do her minions, igniting a communal eros of tantric contortions and thrusts. Yet Jerome, due to a lack of human-approximate anatomy, could only stand inertly and offer loose descriptions of each pose. The results were chaos.

For instance:

– EVERYONE PLEASE TOUCH YOUR TOES! REGARDS, JEROME.

I fell to the ground and, cradling my feet, embarked on an intimate session of 'This Little Pig.' My wife decoded Jerome's imperative as a call to remain standing and touch her toes *to each other*, which resulted in the acrobatic feat of balancing on the outside of her ankles and pressing her feet sole-to-sole. Meanwhile another couple tapped their toes in waltz-time on the grass – touching them, I suppose, to the earth – while some showboating madwoman wrapped her legs around her head and, ostentatiously, crammed both feet in her mouth while her spouse stood nearby and clapped.

Only Tubs and Pudding, I noticed, failed to engage with full fervour. Post-diminishment at the hands of Brad Beard, they fingered each other's toes listlessly, and in their eyes shuddered the dwindling flame of troubled faith. Also, something else was different about them ... Something I couldn't place.

After the Stretching Circle concluded, Jerome assembled us on the steps of the Welcome Centre and announced the Morning Activity: a Group Excursion – led by Jerome himself.

At this my wife's interest piqued, her eyebrows peaked. – Excursion?

– YES, said Jerome. REGARDS, JEROME.

– Out … side?

– YES. REGARDS, JEROME.

– Excellent, said Dr. Dhaliwal.

– We can't bloody wait, I added in a show of matrimonial unity – like the co-pilot acquiescing to a suicide mission alongside his fanatical superior.

Yet secretly I worried where we were headed. My hope was that heavily armoured jeeps, or tanks, would safari us out to view the local fauna from a safe and photogenic distance, and we would return having risked neither life nor limb, nor even nose.

Jerome summoned us to, from his tray, select a set of 'ear buddy' headphones.

– FOR THE AUDIO TOUR, he explained. REGARDS, JEROME.

I inserted mine a bit too robustly; they nudged my eardrums, possibly lodged there for good. Better that, however, than some nearsighted orangutan mistaking them for larvae, swinging out of the trees and gnawing off half my face while chewing them free.

When Jerome next spoke, his voice was inside my head.

– THE EXCURSION BEGINS ANON. REGARDS, JEROME.

He wheeled an about-face and went gliding off around the back of the Welcome Centre. And we were off! Only Tubs and Pudding failed to join our group with commensurate aplomb. Watching them fidget and dawdle at the end of the line, I realized what was different about them: overnight, mutinously, they'd both shaved off their beards.

Down a path we went between some service huts, past the pool's chlorinated reek and spectral shimmer, between the percolating jacuzzi and dribbling outdoor showers, then down some steps and along a flagstone path to a gate with a turnstile, where, with a static zap, we scanned our wristbands and exited the backside of the Retreat, arriving shortly at a sawdust path that wiggled into the trees.

– THE TRAILHEAD, narrated Jerome. REGARDS, JEROME.

– Excellent, enthused one of our fellow travellers.

Fool! The jungle? This Excursion was a suicide mission – to hell. And then I realized it was my spouse who had spoken. So this was my lot – for one, for all – with no choice but to conform. And in we went to our collective, bestial murder, two-by-doomèd-two.

The jungle closed around us. My headphones buzzed emptily. (The audio tour was apparently of the minimalist variety.) I remained on guard, pinning the loose fabric of my robes to my sides and tottering along stiff-legged beside my wife into the island's overgrown undergrowth. Dr. Dhaliwal and I were at the end of the pack, forced to trust the pair next in line – Tubs and Pudding – not to lead us astray.

– Do you know where we're being taken? I whispered.

The two men shook their heads grimly. And then one of them – Tubs? Pudding? – confessed something shocking:

– We're feeling like maybe we want to go home.

– But there's no way off the island, said the other, until the end of Day Ten.

Aghast, I slowed my pace to put a little distance between us. How appalling! How uncouth! Also surely the sort of admission best kept to oneself. Afforded anything and everything anyone could ever want – save this death-march into that verdant abyss – these churlish ingrates were considering jumping ship.

Yet my wife seemed intrigued and nudged ahead to confer with the two rogues in low tones. When she rejoined me, the expression on her face suggested some new tenacity and determination. But for what? Then, as ever, a gulf of existential fundament gaped between us. What was my ostensible beloved after? Who was she, even?

On we walked. Other than the faint hum of some obtuse radio frequency in our headsets, the only sounds were shuffling footsteps. When a squawk resounded off in the trees, Jerome interpreted it sexually:

– A MATING CALL. REGARDS, JEROME.

And on we went, a hushed parade through the bush, to god knows what or where.

Oh: to a village.

The path ended at this village's outer wall, a sixty-foot, turreted fortification. I feared archers or boiling oil. But Jerome simply led our robed convoy up to a gateway to scan our wristbands. A wicket permitted us through and into the town square, where vendors' stalls formed a gridwork of cobblestone laneways. In the centre of this market stood a greenly oxidized copper statue that, at a glance, I identified as the standard conqueror-on-horseback variety, rearing up regally and heralding the subjugation of some less avaricious past.

What the village – or at least the square – seemed to lack was people. Nobody manned the stalls; no local shoppers flitted about; no harangue of bargaineering filled the air. The place was empty. Abandoned? No. This felt like the aftermath of a recent clear-cut, the forest sliced to stumps. Yet an echo of the vibrant past still lingered. Life had been here, recently, and someone, or something, had made it vanish.

– EACH STALL, said Jerome's voice in my headphones, HAS A SCANNER FOR YOUR WRISTBANDS. PURCHASES WILL BE BILLED TO YOUR ACCOUNT. WE WILL LEAVE FROM THE STATUE IN ONE HOUR, EXACTLY. DO NOT BE LATE. REGARDS, JEROME.

Shopping! Souvenirs! Commercial arousal rippled through our two dozen-strong cohort. And then, as if someone had squirted soap into our oily midst, the group scattered. I watched my fellow excursioners assault the stalls with purchases; a chorus of twittering wristbands filled the air. Only my wife, I, Tubs, and Pudding remained, flanking Jerome, unmoved and unmoving.

– PLEASE, said Jerome, BROWSE THE VENDORS' OFFERINGS AT YOUR LEISURE. JUST DON'T LEAVE THE MARKET AND BE BACK BY NOON. REGARDS, JEROME.

– Don't leave the market? said Dr. Dhaliwal. Why?

– … , said Jerome's lights.

Ever the rabble-rouser, Dr. Dhaliwal eyed a bell tower lofting out of the low sandstone buildings outside the square. At the apex of the tower was a crow's nest that afforded views over the town, and perhaps beyond. It was this lookout, I noticed, that entranced my wife most of all.

– PLEASE, said Jerome again, BROWSE THE VENDORS' OFFERINGS AT YOUR LEISURE. JUST DON'T LEAVE THE SQUARE AND BE BACK BY NOON. REGARDS, JEROME.

– Where are the people? asked my wife, removing her headphones.

– PLEASE, repeated Jerome, BROWSE THE VENDORS' OFFERINGS AT YOUR LEISURE. JUST DON'T LEAVE THE SQUARE AND BE BACK BY NOON. REGARDS, JEROME.

I suggested that we could have a look through the market with everyone else, gently attempting to steer my wife by the elbow toward compliance. In truth, I was concerned about Jerome short-circuiting; he seemed built like a pipe bomb.

Dr. Dhaliwal snatched her arm from me.

– Where are the locals, Jerome? Where are the people who live here?

Instead of replying, Jerome rolled away from us, the lights on his head scrolling a sequence of dots. And then with a little triad of descending notes (A, F, D, I believe) the image was replaced by a red, pulsing image of a power cord.

– I believe he's recharging, I said.

– Perfect, said my wife. She turned to Tubs and Pudding, who waited meekly by. You two, have a look around the market, see if you can figure out what's going on. We'll head up that tower, scout the island for a way out, and meet you back here in an hour.

– We? I said.

But she was already on the move, snatching a handful of my robes and dragging me along. – Let's go!

Needless to say, I have never been one for waywardness – civil or uncivil, cultural or sanitary. The rules of law and nature protect me from dangers viral, serpentine, aeronautic, self-inflicted, etc., so I obey them to the letter. Authority shields us naïfs from our own ignorance, stifling the lava of free will inside its mountain of submission. Tell me what to do and how to do it, generally, and I will, lest I find myself erupting in great searing fonts of magma and shame.

No, disobedience has never been 'my personal baggage.' I fail to understand the appeal of the most benign crimes. For example, jesting. I align not with ne'er-do-wells. And yet, as she eyed the bell tower I had to wonder: was my wife the type to never do well? I couldn't imagine it. She was about as well done as anyone – a steak grilled to a blackened husk, a veritable specimen of roasted-through integrity. Her job was *security guard*, for heaven's sake – a paragon of rule-enforcement!

Yet away we strayed from the down-powered Jerome, between stalls of plastic trinkets, plastic tchotchkes, plastic knickknacks and bric-a-bracs, plastic curios and doodads, plastic jewellery inset with plastic stones, plastic fruit, plastic veg, plastic figurines, plastic spades, plastic buckets, plastic rakes, plastic hoes, plastic trowels, plastic shovels, plastic cups, plastic sunhats, plastic water shoes, plastic bats, plastic balls, plastic swords, plastic water pistols, plastic simulated beach glass, plastic flippers and diving masks, plastic disposable cameras, and plastic snowglobes in which raged not blizzards but sandstorms – a nightmare to endure, surely, and a dubious means of commemorating one's holiday: *See how we suffocated at the beach.*

The market had everything, it seemed – except an exit. The whole area was wrapped and bounded with endless sheets of tarpaulin, with no break or exit to the outside world. As we zigged and zagged down the market's alleys, searching for some elusive gap in the boundary, I mewled some meek protestations from behind:

– But! But! But!

Dr. Dhaliwal, heeding me not, barrelled ahead.

At the end of the row she cornered again, accelerating with the graceful power of a stampeding bull, her robes streaming like the intestines of its freshly disembowelled matador. I drafted behind, my breath ragged and raw in my chest. But lo! She was pointing ahead. Was it? Yes! Daylight! Between a stall of souvenir toothbrushes and another of souvenir floss shone a gap bright with sunshine – an escape hatch!

We dove into that narrow slice in the plastic, squeezing through and pushing out jaws-first like freshly breached calves. The guilt of rebellion consumed me as I stumbled into the forbidden territory beyond the market.

– Have we gone, I suggested gently, far enough?

Dr. Dhaliwal responded by nodding at the bell tower a hundred metres ahead to our left. And then we were on the move again, down a narrow laneway lined with sandstone cottages, windows and doors tightly, silently shuttered, lending the place the timeless, lifeless feel of a museum – or a graveyard. Yet the cobblestones beneath our feet were worn smooth as soap. People had lived here, possibly recently. Their whereabouts remained a mystery, but as we pushed deeper, the village felt less abandoned than arrested, as if all human activity here had suddenly been stopped.

The good doctor brought us around a final corner, and there it was: the building with the bell tower. Perhaps not a church or temple, as I noted none of the telltale stained glass, imperious iconography, or fear-mongering artwork (fiendish hellscapes, fire-breathing goats, deranged babies, etc.) that heralded those institutions. Yet that turreted tower ascending forty feet into the air lent the place an officiousness and utility: if not a house of worship, it was a house of *something*.

More peculiarly, in front of the building stood a platform. And upon the platform was a structure that at first I took to be a work of modern sculpture whose codified meaning would be lost on me. But then I reconsidered: the device was clearly an oil derrick paused between slurps of the earth's sweet black lifeblood. No, wait! It was, rather, some sort of pagan talisman, hewn from sacred trees and tilted toward the sun to appeal for heat or light or mercy.

It was Dr. Dhaliwal who refined my interpretations:

– A guillotine, she said.

For a moment even the indomitable Dr. Dhaliwal seemed cowed – not in that she dropped to all fours to chomp grass into cud and low at the moon, but simply that she stilled and quieted and seemed to waver, ever so briefly, in her mission. It was impossible to misinterpret the true, sinister nature of the object before us, with its gleaming blade and blood-soaked neck-cradle scalloped into the structure below – the instrument of a punishment so capital that it sent one's head rolling away like an upper-case O!

Faced with such horrors, I began to reconsider my deference to authority. If alleged criminality could be punished with a beheading – well, my god, what barbarism informed the law? Who were the real monsters? Barbers, certainly, but also legislators, knife sharpeners, murder enthusiasts – as well as us plebians who submit so unquestioningly to the powers-that-be, or -were. I struggled to justify amputation in the name of social order, even of so much as a lowly eyelash. For without eyelashes the human face assumes a disturbing aspect; if the eyes are the windows to the soul, eyes without lashes are windows without shutters: ugly, denuded holes in the skull of your head-house.

When she did edge around the platform, my wife's eyes never left the guillotine, as if it might spring to life and come slashing and chomping at us, and she moved at an uncharacteristically wary shuffle. For once I had no trouble matching her gait, as sidling is as natural to me as the bumble to the bumblebee, or the slink to the devious salamander. Once around the murderous machine we mounted the steps to the building. Cautiously my wife tried the door. I hung back, glancing around the courtyard. But the only sign of life was the distant chirp of our cortege digitally plundering the market.

The handle turned. The door creaked archetypally open.

Inside was hushed and cool, and very dark. We waited in the building's foyer for our eyes to adjust to the gloom. A little light sliced in through some narrow slits high up the stone walls, twirling dust, and I could sense by the echo of the door closing that the ceiling was lofty. We acclimated and the room focused into view: pews! Or perhaps just benches arranged in a congregational fashion with an aisle up the middle. Was this a hall of worship, or theatre, or justice? Perhaps all three? I pictured an eccentric religious rite that incorporated shadow puppetry and interpretive dance and climaxed with a festive beheading on the steps.

– There, said Dr. Dhaliwal.

She was pointing, and now moving, toward an arched doorway on the right side of the hall. The access to the tower, I imagined she imagined. Again I set off after her, as any decent husband might – and should, I think?

My wife was right: beyond the doorway a spiral staircase led up the tower into a lightless oblivion. As she began to ascend – always so brazen! – I eyed the sooty void above. My hand found a wooden banister affixed to the wall and, like a child grasping its parent's hand, clung to it as I toed the first step. Cold stone met my foot. But the banister held, so I kept going: another frigid step, then another. I tried to synchronize my climb with my wife's, but she mounted the tower at a hellbent clip, and the soft padding of her footfalls began to fade as she left me 'eating all of her dust.'

– No rush, I called, chuckling.

– Come on, she replied, her voice misting down to me, vaporous and indistinct.

Such was my lot: the dutiful husband, following behind, ready to catch my wife if she fell. Though Dr. Dhaliwal wasn't the type to fall, and even if she did my chances of saving her were slim, what with my chronic case of Babysitter's Elbow and my propensity, when thrown anything, to duck and shriek rather than attempt a catch. No, were my wife to misstep or trip she'd tumble right through me, sending us both pinwheeling floorward in a tangle of broken limbs and spirits.

At any rate: I seized the banister and strode up the stairs with an approximation of confidence, despite each blind step feeling like it could send me sailing off a precipice.

Though it wasn't the ascent into the dark that troubled me most. As I climbed, the wood began to, I felt, *change* under my hand. Its texture became sinuous, as if not planed properly, with thick, knotted cords twisting to the surface. Still I gripped it, and trod onward and upward, with my wife's footsteps now so faint that I could barely hear them ahead. But after another few steps the banister, bizarrely, seemed to be softening. It felt less wooden now than … like flesh, ropy and muscly.

It felt, I realized, like a neck.

No: like hundreds of necks, stitched end to end and strung up the tower and struggling, as a single organism, to breathe.

A pulse thrummed in it too.

I recoiled.

The banister began making wet, sucking sounds, as if dragging great inhalations down … to what? I shuddered to think what tracheal horrors dwelled below – some monster's undulating gullet; a pair of heaving, leathery lungs. So what then lurked above? I pictured the banister culminating in a huge, toothless mouth the size of a cauldron, gulping at the air at the top of the tower. Wheezing. Ravenous.

Down or up? Both options seemed equally awful. Meanwhile the banister continued to writhe and gasp and gurgle inches away.

– Dr. Dhaliwal? I called feebly into the dark. My darling?

No reply. Only those gulps and that squelchy chugging. And me trapped amid that squelching, sepulchral blackness, with nothing to hold on to.

And then it was over. The lights flicked on. I was in a regular stairwell, with a regular banister not crafted from human throats, but wood, and the steps spiralling regularly inside the tower – up or down, depending which way you faced: such was the subjective paradox of stairs. And I could hear footsteps again, though these seemed to be approaching, not fading away.

I braced myself as they neared – the guillotine operator, I imagined, lugging my wife over his shoulder, to pluck me off my feet and carry us to slaughter in a 'two-Dhaliwals-for-one' extravaganza, our severed skulls clattering like castanets over the cobblestones. Or perhaps what advanced toward me was simply a giant mouth with feet. Regardless, as was often the case in moments of crisis, instead of 'fighting or flighting' I defaulted to 'freezing in place and trying not to weep.'

Whoever was thumping down the stairs was just around the corner. I closed my eyes and braced myself to be kidnapped and decapitated, or massively licked.

– It's worse than I expected, said Dr. Dhaliwal's voice. Let's go.

My wife! She pushed past, leaving me gawking up the tower. What was there?

I met her at the ground-floor landing. Before I could move into the main hall, she arm-barred the way and lifted a finger to her lips. Perplexing. But then I followed her gaze: in the faint light from the tower, I could see that the pews were full – and perhaps always had been. In silent rows sat a hundred-odd penitents – their heads bowed? I could only make out humped shoulders in the gloom. Praying. Why?

Through a crackle of radio interference Jerome's voice exploded in my ears.

– PREPARE TO GATHER. THE EXCURSION ENDS IN FIVE MINUTES. REGARDS, JEROME.

He'd recharged! I glanced at my wife. Her own headphones were nowhere in sight. And neither – shockingly – was her wristband. The flesh where it had wrapped her arm looked purple and raw, puckered in a strange pattern of dots and divots. I eyed my own wrist, realizing that the area beneath that plastic strip was numb. But what was I going to do, chew it free? Besides, we had 'bigger fried fish' with which to deal, and a tardy return to the market risked at best a reprimand – and at worst, what? Death by decapitation?

As I began to warn her, she clamped a hand over my mouth and nodded toward that hushed, hunched congregation, rapt in prayer or meditation or private contemplation. I recognized the repentant posture as one I adopted to catalogue, consider, lament, and apologize for the day's ignominies. Certainly it seemed wrong, if not perilous, to disturb them mid-supplication. Especially when they had ready access to a guillotine.

But, wait! I had the solution. Gently I eased around my wife. She looked bewildered, but also curious. (*Taking the lead? Mr. Dhaliwal?*) But this was no time for her headlong and audacious charge of daring achievement; it would surely be the death of us now. Our safe getaway could only be made with the mousy, shameful, apologetic, but ultimately silent footsteps … of mincing.

My god did I mince! I minced like I'd never minced before: up on tiptoes, body collapsed into a deflated slouch, each delicate step like the sad scuffle of some emotionally bankrupted fairy. And my wife, recognizing a true master, followed my lead. Together we minced behind the pews, through the darkness, toward the stripe of daylight that glowed under the front door, which we reached, thanks to my stealth and preternatural timidity, without a single congregant looking up from their prayers. They were so still, in fact, that I began to wonder if they were living beings at all …

–THE EXCURSION ENDS IN FOUR MINUTES, announced Jerome via my headset, as we reached the main door. REGARDS, JEROME.

I held up four fingers.

Dr. Dhaliwal nodded, seized the handle and held the door open for me (chivalrously) before slipping through herself. Outside the daylight blinded us and we reeled into it like moles, stumbling down the steps past the guillotine, gathering steam and vision as we fled along one lane-way, doglegged onto another, and at last reached the market – but where was the way in? We scurried alongside that tarpaulin border, scanning it for the flap that would permit us inside.

– THE EXCURSION ENDS IN THREE MINUTES, said Jerome. REGARDS, JEROME.

– Three! I cried instructively.

– There! my wife cried anagrammatically.

And she was gone, ducking through a slit in the barrier. Like a belated, fraternal twin I slid in after her. Reunited, our 'tails high,' we galloped apace back to the market's central square. As we joined the group, Jerome regarded my wife and me expressionlessly – perhaps, to be fair, due to his lack of a face.

– THE EXCURSION ENDS IN TWO MINUTES, he seemed to sigh. REGARDS, JEROME.

Everyone but us toted plastic bags of plastic odds and ends; the more enterprising shoppers had procured plastic laundry baskets they'd stuffed to the brims. That we lacked purchases felt like proof of our sedition. Jerome's timer ticked down, each second labouring through our peers' scrutiny: What sort of people were these, I sensed them wondering, who failed to shop on a shopping trip? Monsters, surely. Possibly heretics.

– THE EXCURSION ENDS IN ONE MINUTE, said Jerome. REGARDS, JEROME.

And then I felt a nudge – Tubs, elbowing me. Or was it Pudding?

– Here, he whispered, handing me a pair of mirrored sunglasses.

Amid the darkened vista of these 'shady specs,' experiencing the world as Brad Beard did – without all the insights and catchphrases and merchandising opportunities, of course – I noticed that Tubs' or Pudding's counterpart, Pudding or Tubs, had likewise donated a pair of sunglasses to my wife. Yet I worried that instead of helping us pass for shopping enthusiasts we looked secretive and dubious, like fugitives or terrorists.

The time was up. A green checkmark illuminated Jerome's head.

– THE EXCURSION IS OVER, he announced. REGARDS, JEROME.

One at a time we were ushered through the wicket, each wristband scanned and accounted for with a robotic chirp and attendant electric shock. I worried that my wife would be trapped, yet cannily she had retained the remains of her own wristband and when it was her turn dangled it before the sensor – and was allowed out. I was next, but before I left the village, I looked back at that statue in the middle of the town square.

I shuddered. This was not, I realized, an oxidized sculpture of some valiant conqueror rearing back on a mighty stallion.

It was, in fact, just a big pile of green, desiccated heads.

Session #3 Transcript

– Ah, Dr. and Mr. Dhaliwal, how good, as always, to see you, today, please close the door, and take a seat, as we embark upon, would you believe, already, our third Session, which, as you will discover, is going to be, perhaps, a bit different, I think, from our previous Sessions, as, today, we will be, if you'll pardon the expression, shaking things up, a bit, at least, that is, from our regular format, and, if we might proceed immediately, if that's all right with you, may I ask, are you familiar with, as it's known, Erotic Role Play?

– With dice?

– No, Mr. Dhaliwal, that would be *roll*, R-O-L-L, and, while some might find the homonym confusing, what I mean is, specifically, *role*, as in R-O-L-E.

– Ah.

– Yes, all right, then, so, Mr. Dhaliwal, please think of this, if you will, as a kind of game, orchestrated by me, and in which you, Dr. and Mr. Dhaliwal, are the Erotic Role Players, by which I mean, specifically, that you will be each playing a Role, that is, a Role who is not yourself, but one adopted, inhabited, and, yes, played.

– Ah, yes. Like acting.

– Well, perhaps, Mr. Dhaliwal, we might think of Erotic Role Play as similar to acting, in that you, both, adopt the characteristics of some other person, real or imagined, or even animal, with the goal, that is, of assuming an alternate identity, for yourself, which, in some way, captures the essence of who you are, and then, collectively, you play these Roles in an Erotic Fantasy Scenario, which I concoct, script, direct, observe, interpret analytically, and the results of which will, in effect, advance your Treatment.

– An animal? For example a frog?

– A, was it, *frog*, Mr. Dhaliwal?

– Yes. I'd like to be a frog.

– Well, certainly, Mr. Dhaliwal, if *frog* is the Role that feels, as it were, closest to who you are, be that today, or, perhaps, in some intrinsic and essential way, then, yes, you may certainly, if it pleases you, Erotic Role Play as a *frog*, today, in our session.

– Ribbit.

– Yes, excellent, Mr. Dhaliwal, that's the spirit, and, may I say, what extraordinary tongue work, and I wouldn't want to be a fly, literally, on the wall, wow, faced with such lingual vigour, not to mention your squat posture, and, so, Dr. Dhaliwal, if your husband has, I believe, selected *frog* as his Role, what, may I ask, would be your choice, today, of what you would, complementarily, like to be, that is, in this Erotic Role Play?

– Steamroller.

– Quite, if I may say so, a curious choice, Dr. Dhaliwal, when your husband –

– Ribbit.

– Yes, thank you, Mr. Dhaliwal – has opted for the Role of *frog*, so why not perhaps consider the Role of, for example, *other frog*, or *lady frog*, or *companionate frog*, or *toad*, or even *fly*, for which the tongue of your husband's frog might express rapacious longing?

– Growl.

– Fine then, Dr. Dhaliwal, despite my protestations I must recognize the sound of your engines, as it were, warming up, though I would be remiss, as your counsellor, if I failed to mention, briefly, that you have both assumed Roles, *frog* and *steamroller*, quite suddenly, and, to be frank, independently, even separately, and, dare I say, individualistically, when a successful Erotic Role Play is, typically, best concocted in collaboration, that is, together, between the two of you, so that I might, accordingly, concoct a harmonious, and appropriately erotic, Erotic Fantasy Scenario.

– Ribbit.

– Growl.

– Ribbit!

– Please, Mr. Dhaliwal, there's no need to hop behind the couch, your wife isn't, I don't believe, going to run you over, and flatten you to a green paste, and I assume, Dr. Dhaliwal, that your steamroller is of the sort, one hopes, that is *friendly* to frogs, and a confirmation, Dr. Dhaliwal, that you aren't, now, going to flatten your husband to a green paste might, perhaps, comfort him, and coax him out, that is, from behind the couch, so that this Erotic Role Play might, per its intention, explore the erotic dynamics of your relationship, and not, as it currently seems, the capacity of one of you, Dr. Dhaliwal, to flatten the other, Mr. Dhaliwal, to a green paste.

– Growl.

– Ribbit!

– No, please, wait, both of you, don't move, give me a moment, while I concoct an appropriate Erotic Fantasy Scenario that features, confoundingly, a *frog* and a *steamroller*, and which can't, one hopes, end with the frog being flattened to green paste, but rather –

– Ribbit?

– Please, Mr. Dhaliwal, for the love of god, shut up, I require silence, it's incredibly difficult to focus –

– Growl.

– Dr. Dhaliwal, please, flattening your husband, the frog, into a green paste, is hardly erotic at all.

– Growl.

– Ribbit?! Ribbit!

– All right, enough, perhaps we should, simply, abandon this Erotic Role Play –

– Growl. Growl, growl, growl.

– Ribbit, ribbit, ribbit!

– Growl, growl, growl!

– For the love of god, Dr. and Mr. Dhaliwal, there's no need to –

– Ribbit!

Ribbit! Ribbit!

– Please, please, no, this isn't –

– Grrrrrrrrrrrooooooooooooooowwwwwwwwwwwl.

– Rib … bit.

– Crunch, growl, smear, growl, splat, growl, crunch.

– *Croak.*

Four

That night, after the tidal gyrations of my watery bed had settled, I waited for my wife to 'join me' – not biblically, nor even physically, but merely on the adjacent floor. Instead she stood in the middle of the room, a shadow upright and motionless in the dark.

– Goodnight? I ventured.

– Shhh, she said.

– Shall we discuss the events of the day?

– Events?

– Your … excursion. Up the tower? What, dare I ask, did you discover there?

Yet we were disrupted by a surge from the television: here came the nightly instructional video in all its lurid glory. Over the set my wife draped her bath towel, mostly concealing the visual spectacle, and spoke through its husky, mewling, squelching soundtrack in the tone of lament:

– This place isn't okay. They're … *up to things.* I think there's a plan for everyone – anyway, don't worry. You keep playing along. I'm going to find a way out.

I thumbed my wristband, which seemed to have fused to my skin, hoping my wife didn't expect me to hack it off collusively. I dreaded being embroiled in some conniving scheme, perhaps one requiring disguises, coded messages, the secreting of a microfiche inside an orifice. But no commands followed; only the TV moaned. Dr. Dhaliwal relapsed into silence, her coiled posture less inert than poised and preparatory. For what?

Safer not to know. Her instructions were to *play along* – my life's work! As a child, when hurled into the reedy depths of the orphanage's pond, I'd surface spawn-slathered and giggle amiably at my classmates: what fun! Boys shall be cruel, hilarious boys! So if my wife's incipient rebellion required me to maintain conformity, I could certainly support her. I rolled over, waited for my sloshing mattress to still, and tried, per the nocturnal conventions of the Retreat, and society, to sleep.

Just as I was drifting off, the click of our door opening snatched me back into consciousness. I hid under the bedding, anticipating the incoming lurch of something hornily vampiric or otherwise undead, some licentious succubal beast summoned by the moon to sup at our jugulars – or to drag us into the jungle for a midnight frolic. But there was no telltale scuttle of talons across the floorboards. Only silence.

I peeked over the top of my sheets. The room, save my own corpus, was empty. The TV was off.

And my wife was gone – slipped away into the night.

Her mission, whatever it was, had begun.

The next morning, I was roused from a fitful, lurching sleep by a chorus of voices parading past my hut, boasting ravenously.

  – I'm so hungry I could eat a horse!

  – I'm so hungry I could eat a mule!

  – I'm so hungry I could eat a leg!

  – I'm so hungry I could eat two men's arms!

  – I'm so hungry I could eat the arms of two men, i.e., all four arms!

  – I'm so hungry I could eat your ears!

  – I'm so hungry I could eat your teeth!

  – I could eat my own mouth!

  – My whole face!

  – Everyone's face!

  – Everyone's face with a ketchup of blood!

  – Blood ketchup on a leaf, four newspapers, and a rocking chair!

  – All that plus dessert!

  – A dessert of splinters, broken glass, and nails!

  – Carpenter's nails?

  – *Human* nails.

My wife was still missing. And breakfast, it seemed, was being served.

I arrived alone at the dining hall and, with a wary look at my wristband, electrocuted myself through the turnstiles. All the other couples were filling their plates – paired and dutiful. Some even lovingly moistened each other's cereals with milk, portending Sayer-approved 'afternoon matinees.' Yet my wife had abandoned me, ergo the sacrament of marriage, and I stood at the head of that great smorgasbord as bereft as the dateless, drunk uncle who estranges every wedding.

Though perhaps the good doctor was only attending to her morning toilet and would be right along, lickety-split? Which made this an opportunity for gallantry. Yes! A chance to assume the manly duties of food-gathering and chivalrously shine. Then Dr. Dhaliwal would arrive freshly washed, powdered, lotioned, and creamed to a breakfast of continental proportions. I snatched up a plate and set to it: double-dosings of eggs! sausages! pancakes! bacons! Suzette's crêpes! a Frenchman's toast! a Frenchman's fries! puddings of butterscotch and blood! jams and marmalades and jellies and condiments! syrup! coffee, tea, drinking chocolate, a 'fruitée smoothée'!

Emerging triumphantly from that alimentary gauntlet, I spied Tubs and Pudding and with my teeming plate made 'like a line of bees' to the back corner of the room.

The two men sat grimly before what, I realized as I sat, was not a selection from the buffet but a great slurry of refuse. Churned to a pulp amid organic scraps (fish bones, meat trimmings, various peels, rinds, skins, etc.) were dirt, bark, leaves, and twigs. A sprinkling of sand. Some pebbles. Seashell fragments. Moss. A shard of soap. A tangle of hair. Unidentifiable clippings. Scrunched, stained tissues. And was that … something's lip?

The vile concoction gleamed with a glossy, mucosal sheen that suggested the stomach-slicked regurgitations of some indiscriminate and regretful omnivore – a goat starved to savagery or a particularly stupid whale. Also the fellows' brunch, such as it was, seemed to tremble with an aura of menace, as if it might lurch from the dishware and seize one of us wetly by the face.

Yet the beardless lovers gazed at that unpalatable mess with resignation.

Quickly I shoved my own breakfast in their direction.

– Regard, gents! While we wait for my esteemed better half, please feel free to share with me this fine, exquisitely curated, and eminently edible meal!

But Tubs and Pudding, whichever Beard had christened as which, shook their heads.

– We've had enough of that sort of thing, said one of them – Tubs, possibly.

– We're thinking differently now, affirmed his husband (Pudding? Or maybe Tubs?).

And then they swept up their knives and forks. What quivered before them seemed the result of a morning spent rooting through the retreats' dumpsters: a concoction of pure, abhorrent waste.

– Gentlemen, please, I sputtered. You can't be serious. That's not even food!

Up came the cutlery.

– It's perfectly edible, said, perhaps, Pudding.

– It's better this way, said the other – perhaps Tubs.

I wanted to cry out, to leap up, to dance a discouraging jig, to seize my friends' hands before they could tuck into that plateful of rubbish. Yet their forbearance paralyzed me. Where would they begin? With a slice of mud? A forkful of fur?

My god – they were tucking in!

In perfect, seemingly rehearsed synchronicity Tubs and Pudding eased their forks into the variegated mush and steadied their knives adjacently. So measured, so methodical. So tender! Almost loving.

Upon their forks the knives smeared shreds of a sodden napkin, some scales, a feather, a globule of lard, a flap of flesh …

I looked away.

And looked back! Repulsive, certainly. But also riveting.

The forks lifted, drizzling murky fluids; the waiting mouths yawed. The guck approached.

I couldn't watch!

I could!

The mess vanished between the men's lips. They both winced – at the textures? the flavours? I expected regurgitation. Instead they chewed. And swallowed. And their forks returned for more. And more. Again, and again, until the white of the plate began to reappear.

Through this shocking performance Tubs and Pudding's faces remained mostly expressionless. This wasn't eating, I thought, watching them inhale another gelatinous, gurgling mouthful; I was witnessing some sort of diabolical ritual.

They were scraping up the final leavings now, a sort of mucky goo.

Then it was over. They sat back. Together we eyed my own, heaped plate. Suddenly it, too, had the look of not food, but slop. My stomach turned. I nudged it across the table, out of arm's reach. And sat back, gazing around the dining hall, at all that glorious excess so brazenly amassed and consumed: soon enough, it too would become waste.

No! What thoughts were these?

Dr. Dhaliwal had told me to *keep playing along* (viz., to normalcy). Instead, I'd turned spectator to a garbage-eating game played by apostates.

I couldn't associate myself with such unconvention. My wife had given me a purpose: social decorum. To act as regular as a plainly salted potato crisp; to fit in! My presence at the Retreat was already tenuous. In addition to my stolen identity, I'd now breakfasted with this pair of rubbish-guzzling oddballs. And done so solo, sans spouse. And to be single at a couples' retreat was, inarguably, weird.

After breakfast, I joined Jerome's Stretching Circle with ambitions of conformity, yet felt conspicuously atypical as I writhed around solo in the grass. All around me loving duos slid through their postures like two-headed chimera. Not only did my wife fail to show, but Tubs and Pudding abdicated too, slinking off to their hut. And all three turncoats were also conspicuously absent from the subsequent Morning Activity: 'Takin' it Ease: A Group Meditation Narrated by Brad Beard.'

Still without partner, on the walk over to the Retreat's Leisure Sector I sidled up to a couple whose beards looked freshly painted on. Despite their cordiality – my blazing grin was returned with polite nods – my vain attempt at 'three-wheeling' was thwarted when we got to the hammocks: the two women selected one, climbed deftly aboard and, with no room for a third, left me derelict on the grass. Before Brad Beard could single me out pedantically, I dove into a nearby number strung up between two frondy palms. My technique was too propulsive; the thing swallowed me like a maw. Thrashing my way up for air, I sent my cloth coffin teetering pendulously, the trees that held it aloft groaning in protest or, perhaps, embarrassment.

Clearly these hammocks were designed for two. With no wife to counterbalance the weight, 'Takin' it Ease' would be impossible. Never mind my general predilection for takin' everything every way except for ease: with unease, primarily, but also hard.

Here was Beard, facial hair luminous with wax and balm.

– Welcome, welcome, everyone, he began, slick and brassy as a greased trombone. That's it, get comfortable, all of you. Can you feel the Trunity in the air this morning? I can almost smell it. Am I right?

A great sniff and purr of assent came floating out of the hammocks, while mine tossed about like a dinghy in a typhoon.

– Here's a chance, via group relaxation, to really maximize your Core Principles, continued Beard. Just listen to the smooth jazz of my voice, follow my instructions, and you'll find yourselves slipping into what I like to terminologize the Third State: a state of bliss, harmony, and the likes of Trunity you've never imagined imagining.

A strange, glittery sound followed. I peeked over the edge of my pendulous hammock. Beard, robes cascading biblically, was straddling a harp and, with a masseur's tenderness, tickling from it the glittery percolations of gently burped cherubim. Heavenly.

– To begin, I want you all to imagine that you're just one big splat of aspic. All of you, all together. That's it. No bones, no flesh, everything just melted down into trembling slime. Doesn't that feel good?

Beard strummed a chord. At last my hammock stilled, clutching me like a chrysalis.

– So you're jelly. All of you. And you can't quite figure out where what was once your body stops and the person beside you's begins, or the next person either. You're all just one big gooey mush. A kind of ooze. No thoughts, no worries, no cares, no words. Just nothing. Except maybe sugar and water and boiled bones. And that? You feel that? Like a kind of wormy wiggle through your soul? It's … *Trunity* – isn't it?

Preventing me from fully engaging with Beard's mantric oration was a tropical bird, all garish plumage and razory beak, which surveyed me from the branches above with a gloating, predatory look. Was this the type to feast on men? I envisioned it looping lazily up from its roost before diving downward with all the precision and velocity of a cruise missile, plucking both of my eyes from their sockets and then soaring off for a juicy ocular snack among the clouds.

So between this lurid avian threat, an innate inability to relax, the claustrophobic seizure of my solo-piloted hammock and, having forgone breakfast, my plummeting blood sugar, I couldn't commit to Beard's gelatinous fantasia. I was a man, not a marmalade!

Would a wife have helped? A companion? Undoubtedly. Especially the stalwart Dr. Dhaliwal. But where in blazes was she? And what was she up to, wherever that be?

My thoughts, and Beard's harp-tickling, were interrupted with wailing. A siren, I assumed – air-raid or air-rescue. I sat up, ready to debark for cover or escape.

Except this was no siren. The piercing shriek that, frankly, ruined our collective ease-takin' was the wailing of a man.

Tubs or Pudding staggered into our midst, sobbing inconsolably. And, more notably, almost as naked as the day he was born (unless he came into the world wearing a wristband). Whichever half of the Tubs-Pudding conglomerate this was, he collapsed to his knees, keening and hollering as if emotionally drawn-and-quartered.

Brad Beard kicked aside his harp, wrenched loose an empty hammock, and draped it over the weeping man, sparing us the frenzied, mauve spectacle of his nether regions (while denying us the platonic spectacle of his carved musculature). Yet still he wailed, summoning Jerome, who wheeled up with a heart shape pulsing upon his head-screen, and then Professor Sayer, notepad at the ready (ever the pro, wow).

Gradually Tubs or Pudding's sobs quieted to faint blubbering. Brad Beard crouched beside him, whispering sweet, pro bono nothings in his ear. Sayer sidled in, scribbling – what? Observations, prognoses, analyses? Or perhaps charcoal sketches of a man in the throes of grief? Meanwhile Jerome's digital heart pulsed in compassion and 2/4 time.

Just when we'd all believed his hysterics to have reached their end, Tubs/Pudding unleashed a forlorn, primal scream – a terrific, mournful keening of pure grief, of absolute loss, of total desolation, and tore free from his hammock-cassock, genitalia unleashed in renewed turmoil.

– He's dead, screamed Tubs or Pudding. Dead!

– *He must mean his husband Pudding,* whispered someone from a nearby hammock.

– *No, I think that one's Pudding,* suggested someone else.

– *Well Tubs then,* replied the first person. *What do I look like, a g-darn name detective?*

And then, mercifully, the bereaved nudist collapsed, into silence, upon the grass.

The body was – how best to put this? Empty.

Gored. Hollowed. Not just gutted: excavated. Split up the middle and scooped out like a pumpkin. No bones, no organs, no internal vessels or tissues or fabrics remained, all of it removed with surgical precision, leaving only a rubbery casing of skin, spatchcocked and left for carrion at the doorstep of Tubs and Pudding's hut. And this withered flesh-sack was also headless. What once had been a man resembled now an unpacked duffel, or a collapsed tent, or a gross bedsheet, or a wrinkly tablecloth, or industrial-grade coveralls, or a great deal of rawhide, or a reeking leather sleeping bag left to vent in the sun.

   – THIS APPEARS TO BE A CASE OF MURDER, announced Jerome. REGARDS, JEROME.

Anxious, aroused muttering splattered through the crowd. The living member of Tubs/Pudding (still unclear which one had 'gotten it' and which one was still 'getting down') shrieked and fell again into the arms of Brad Beard, who patted his head twice and transferred him to the expert counsel of Sayer. The Professor, cooing paratactically, began smoothing out the man's hammock-robe.

The rest of us stood around in a loose semicircle. I sensed my peers' collective gaze shifting from the desiccated, decapitated victim to the surviving half of the couple, to yours truly, and attendantly from horror, through pity, to suspicion. It was my wife, after all, who had been missing all morning. Jerome's shrewd deduction of homicide implied a killer among us. Per the glares and stares, the tutting and clucks, the shaking heads, the pointing fingers, the accusatory whispers, a prime suspect had emerged – and I was being vilified by proximity to said suspect. Perhaps even implicated too.

I had to act fast.

Leaping across the circle, I hauled Tubs/Pudding from the arms of Sayer and consumed him in my own embrace.

– There, I said, there.

I hoped petting his hair in an archetypal gesture of condolence would force reconsiderations about my guilt. How could someone so concerned for the bereaved be involved in murder – or even call a murderer his spouse?

Yet somehow the response turned even more dubious: eyes narrowed, jaws dropped, and rekindled misgivings whisked through the group like a malevolent breeze.

– Oh, Tubbing, I said, smearing the two names together to cover my bases. Dear, terrible Tubbing. Clearly what you need right now is a 'stiffening drink.'

He pulled back – though I held him, unrelentingly, by the hammockrobe. His eyes looked stunned and helpless. Slowly he nodded. – Maybe, yes, he said vaguely.

– That's the spirit, I cried and, as Tubbing's one true friend, swept my 'main man' under my arm to lead him away.

But before we were clear of the scene, he broke free, snatched up the epidermal scraps of his beloved, and slung them like a great sheet over his shoulders. Then he took his (ex-) husband's deflated hands, which had the look of kid-leather gloves, and knotted them at his throat. The fingers, I noted, were also missing.

– Okay, declared Tubbing, outfitted in this flesh-cape. Let's go.

The walk to the Welcome Centre was silent, but no one followed us, and Tubbing's new cloak flapped behind us like a flag in the faint breeze. While the intricacies of the hallways baffled me, Tubbing boasted an admirable sense of direction and led us past the Beauty Realm and Games Room – to the publican house-cum-discotheque, BAR.

I deposited Tubbing onto a stool, his cape draping limply down his back, and straddled the one beside it. A wristband scanner sat before us, as well as an elaborate computerized system for ordering; apparently one simply keyed in a request and the results came spouting from the taps. Science!

– Thirsty? I asked, nodding at the backlit liquors glowing behind the bar.

I was no 'boozing hound-dog.' (My last dalliance with alcohol, on a trip to the zoo, ended tragically – a fire in the hippo enclosure, meat for a year.) Yet there was no better substance to oil the wheels of camaraderie, and I needed Tubbing greased like a con man's unicycle to cement our bond and, concordantly, acquit the Dhaliwals of any wrongdoing.

So I had no choice but to hoist the devil's chalice. To nip a sip of Satan's sin-sap. To swill a dram of DJ (demon-juice), regret-nectar, forgetting-sauce. To do the snoozy-boozy and tip a cuppa wet nasty. To get down with the old slosh-and-tosh, the dupe-lube, the Ol' Knee Buckler. To gore myself with the Knife of Long Nights. I knew how it would go: each deleterious sip would hasten our moral slackening, liquefy our words and limbs, prompt unsolicited confessions and unwanted confidences, elicit shamelessness and incite shame, all the way to tomorrow morning's Early-Hurly: a one-way ticket to Pukeville, population two.

Movement startled me from a table in the shadowy corner of the room. At first all I could make out was beard – and an adjacent throbbing presence. Then faces formed amid the gloom … My god, Beard and Sayer had followed us here – why? To expose my 'tattletale heart'? Perhaps they expected me, delirious with drink, to unload a confession upon my recently widowed companion. But I intended no such thing! And while my wife's behaviour – and disappearance – might be characterized as dubious, she didn't strike me as a murderer. Tubs and Pudding had been her allies!

Even so, it was clear where suspicion lay. Brad Beard lifted his glass ironically in my direction, while Sayer puckered her lips, ran her tongue around them, and blew me a kiss. Yet her eyes were slits. Then these two powerbrokers dipped back into the shadows to whisper. About? Me? My missing wife? It was like guessing the table talk of the gods.

Meanwhile Tubbing had ordered us matching glasses of something pink and sizzling; ice cubes jostled upon the bubbles with the knock of dry bones.

– I would like to make a toast, he said, tears filling his eyes, to the man I loved more than any man has ever loved another man, or woman, or a woman has loved a man, or a woman. Or any other permutation of gender and love one might imagine: our love was more than that, I think, probably.

– Amen, I said, and hummed an *om* for good measure.

Here he lifted his cape and pressed his lips to where the dead fellow's face would have been, yet, severed at the neck, was just a shoddy rubber flap.

– My darling! From the day we met I knew we would be as one, forever. Do you remember? At the police auction? You accused me of undermining your bid on some trowels, and within hours we were engaged. Now I'll wear you until the day I die.

I raised my eyebrows: impressive commitment.

Tubbing lifted his glass in the gesture I recognized as 'a cheers.'

So I smeared my glass against his for the requisite three-count.

And retrieved it, and sipped.

My god! What pink magic had this widowed sorcerer conjured in our cups? I sipped again: superb! Sweet, sour, bitter, but none too much of any one thing, as brilliantly harmonized as a string quartet arriving from four registers upon some unsuspected but vitally satisfying final chord. The nose revealed bubble-gum, lingonberry, and cinnamon, which proceeded into a summer breeze gusting the faraway trills of a child's carefree laughter. This opened into the unmistakable effervescence of hope, which shifted into bittersweet nostalgia, before concluding with the faintest, melancholy hint of quince.

– What spell have you cast upon these waters, friend?

– That? said Tubbing shyly. Just a vodka-cranberry.

– Well my god, man! It's marvellous.

We drank, then held out our empty glasses for the machine to fill us up. I no longer cared that Beard and Sayer might be plotting my capture and arrest – not when heaven overflowed my cup! I felt a splendid loosening within, as if the rigid coil that bound my soul were unspooling with every sip. And now my second drink was gone, too – another!

Another!

Another!

I'm not sure how long we'd been at it – tottering off our stools, giggling, words oozing like fat juicy apricots from our mouths, vision blurred, bodies fuzzy and loose and warm, the splendour only occasionally ruined by great seizures of Tubbing's grief – before Professor Sayer arrived beside us. I sensed her presence before I saw or smelled it: a stiffening of the air, an erection of the wind. She forwent any cordial greeting and gave us a command: an emergency Session, yes, to intervene, immediately, in what appeared, in her professional estimation, to be a crisis, was imperative.

Tubbing and I slid from our stools. And Sayer corralled us down the hall to her office, closed the door, turned on her tape recorder, seated us on her couch, and began.

Session #4 Transcript

– Well, gentlemen, I trust that your state, that is, of intoxication, will afford us some particularities, and possibilities, perhaps otherwise inaccessible, due to your inhibitions, in the therapeutic process, and might I also, if I may, suggest, now, that if either if you are feeling, how to put this, *constrained*, then I, for one, will certainly not judge you, at all, if you choose, at any point, to disrobe.

– Professor, I'm so drunk I can barely see, but are you suggesting we denude?

– Yes, Mr. Dhaliwal, precisely, by which I mean, if I might clarify, that should you feel, due to the amount of alcohol you've consumed, clearly, or the heat in my office, perhaps, the need to, either of you, remove any clothing, be that robes, hammocks worn as robes, or capes, I will neither judge, nor hold against you, the need to liberate your bodies to, as it were, breathe, from the oppression, if one might call it that, of clothing.

– My husband is dead, dead and gone. Dead!

– Yes, Mr. Tubbing, my dear, I know it might seem that way, sometimes, yet dare I point your attention to the, if not 'fine,' than certainly adequate fellow beside you, and wouldn't he make a tolerable replacement, perhaps even on an interim basis, until you find someone, shall we say, better, for why be alone, there's no reason ever to be alone?

– Who's Mr. Tubbing?

– Professor, again, I might be delirious with drink, but are you suggesting that my friend Tubbing and I form a romantic union? This seems disturbing, and rash, when I am already equipped with a wonderful wife, the pluckily autonomous Dr. Dhaliwal – currently indisposed, albeit not suspiciously so.

– Please, Mr. Dhaliwal, your humility is a poor mask for raging insecurity, yet your Treatment simply won't be effective, nor can it continue, if you refuse to accept the obvious crisis between you and your new lover, here, through which I might guide healing, only, I think, yes, via, as I've suggested, nudity.

– You can't heal the murder of my beloved!

– Sorry, Professor – *new* lover?

– One moment, Mr. Dhaliwal, let's, first, Mr. Tubbing, explore that instinct, this alleged, and surely symbolic, *murder*, whether it represents something spiritual and, perhaps, ongoing, with you witnessing, for example, let's say, the slow, spiritual death of your lover, Mr. Dhaliwal, the man seated here beside you, per the overwhelming crush of his inadequacies, under which he is so obviously suffocating and suffering, yes, a kind of murder, or, perhaps, conversely, you feel the murderous capacity of some external force upon him, and your relationship, be it social, cultural, political, sensual, sexual, erotic, oral, anal, what have you, and, again, as I notice you both perspiring so heavily, please, do not feel ashamed if you need to, for example, disrobe, and, look, just to break the ice, why don't I go ahead and take mine off first, there, you see, there's nothing to be ashamed of, though perhaps we would feel more solidarity if, for example, I came and sat with you on the couch, and helped you remove your own?

– Professor, this might be the alcohol clouding my thoughts, but to be clear: this man and I are not in love, merely friends. Anything further would hardly be appropriate when, per its tepid droop over his shoulders, the poor fellow's husband's body is still warm.

– My darling is gone! Gone! Forever gone!

– Shush, gentlemen, please, just let me slide in here between you, doesn't that hand on your thigh feel nice, Mr. Tubbing, let's enjoy ourselves, and, of course, not to exclude you, Mr. Dhaliwal, there, I have two hands for a reason, share the wealth, as they say, now no one's left out, but what's this cape, Mr. Tubbing, surely there's no need for it, now, with all of us sitting so cosily, and the heat, wow, is it hot in here, or is it just me?

– Don't you dare touch him!

– Certainly, Mr. Tubbing, if you'd like to orchestrate things, please, be my guest, I am just as happy to play the subordinate, so if you'd like to leave that cape on, why not, it could add a certain flavour, a certain spice, I'm not averse to the darker erotic arts.

– Thank you. Okay.

– Mr. Tubbing, perhaps, if we are to proceed into, shall we say, more adventurous play, may I suggest a safe word, at this point, to establish some boundaries, and ensure consent, and, if I may, I find that *arugula* has a certain, I think, nice ring to it –

– Arugula? I do like leaves.

– Yes, certainly, that's the spirit, we can ease into things, thank you for relinquishing, was it, your previous kung fu stance, unless what you're into is, as they say, roughing it up a bit, and so, as such, shall I fetch a belt?

– My dear Professor, if I may interject: Is the room spinning? Have we loosed ourselves from gravity into orbit? I hope no one minds if I lie on the floor and close my eyes for a moment … There we are … Very plush carpet … Thank you … Goodnight.

– Mr., sorry, Dhaliwal, are you, is it, sleeping?

– zzz …

– Ah, a sexsomniac, which, I suppose, leaves me and you, Mr. Tubbing, to have at it unfettered by neurotic thirds, so, to begin, come, let me hold you, fall into my arms, that's it, don't be afraid, it's all part of your Treatment, this is how you heal and begin again.

– You'll just hold me? Close? And I won't feel so sad?

– As close as you need, Mr. Tubbing, that's it, at least loosen that silly cape, rest your head upon my bosom, there we are, and, no pressure, we'll see where things lead.

Somehow I was transported to my hut, where I slept the rest of the afternoon, waking groggily at six to the dinner bell, and then simply asleep again. After some time, a throbbing sound infiltrated my dreams: a steady pulse in the deeper recesses of the bass register, like the heartbeat of some massive, dormant beast.

The drums of justice? The knock of an incipient hangover? Both, somehow?

My subconscious extrapolated a dream from this soundtrack: Brad Beard, shirtless and warpainted with the blood of bested rivals (or whatever meat was on hand), thumping the kettledrum of Jerome's head with his fists, eyes glittering with some inner demonic light. A conflagration, thirty feet high, raged in front of the Welcome Centre, and the various couples of the Retreat cavorted nakedly around it to Brad Beard's seismic percussions. Beyond the bonfire a hooded Professor Sayer lorded over the guillotine – and there was Dr. Dhaliwal, my wife, in cuffs, awaiting her fate.

– No, I cried, startling myself awake.

The room was dark. Even the TV remained silent.

From somewhere close, the drumbeat continued.

I roused myself, cracked the door of my hut, peered outside. No fire, no craven ceremony. No sign of my wife, or Tubbing, or Beard, or Sayer, or anyone. Yet, atop the hill, the Welcome Centre blazed with light; somewhere within its labyrinthine passageways, I realized, was the source of that steady, persistent throbbing.

The sound amplified as I crept up the path and into the Welcome Centre, summoning me past the desolate Games Room, and the Beauty Realm, past BAR – that vile if delicious den of iniquity! – until I arrived at the Arts & Entertainment Hub, where the beat clouted the air with such vehemence that it jostled my organs against my ribcage. Warily I crept up to the doors and peeked inside.

The amphitheatre seating was full. The curtains were drawn (that is, closed). That low, almost threatening bass note thundered and growled from speakers on either side of the stage, where, spotlit like a regular Brad Beard, stood Jerome. Singing – still nasally, but in the voice of a sinusitic angel – the final line of what seemed to have been a rousing, well-received one-man (or one-column) overture:

– THE THING'S THE PLAY, WHEREIN JEROME WILL CATCH THE KILLER CONSCIENTIOUSLY, he warbled.

Then he simply stood there, a pillar of rectitude in the light, as the drums crescendo'd until sound puffed from the speakers, blurring the air. Then everything came crashing down in a deafening explosion, which boomed and roared and faded, gradually, into a low drone. Then that quieted too, leaving behind it a silence that swelled from the stage and galloped massively through the room to consume me at the door, like a flame or a wave or a giant thing's hand.

Then the sign-off, as the curtains were drawn (open) and applause sluiced the room.

– REGARDS, JEROME.

Standing upon the stage in tableau were Brad Beard, Professor Sayer, and, shockingly, Tubbing. All were in the standard robes of the Retreat, but Tubbing no longer sported the skin-cape of his beloved. In fact, there was something distinctly un-Tubbing-like about his appearance – not something I could put my finger on, or even near; this proverbial finger merely probed vaguely toward some murky shape in the dark, like a stupefied caterpillar foraging through porridge for its mate.

Beard, meanwhile, seemed at once unlike himself and eerily familiar. His chest, normally thrust outward in a display of masculine hubris, now sank inward like a collapsed balloon. In fact the entire, usual puffery of his demeanour seemed deflated; he withered with all the diffident shame of … Oh dear. That skulk of self-defeat was uncanny and undeniable. I knew it too well. He was acting the part of yours truly (i.e., me).

I only had to glance at Sayer to place the tilt of her jaw, the fixity of her gaze, the severity to her ponytail: pure Dr. Dhaliwal. The Professor had acutely captured my wife's ironic glower, poised insouciance, and tautened forehead, her hair swept back like a flow of magma arrested by nuclear winter.

And Tubbing? He was playing the role of his former beloved. To be fair, the two men were so eerily similar I doubt they owned a mirror. Yet the blocking of the three figures suggested his victimhood: Tubbing, portraying his spouse moments before his death, knelt with his arms raised in self-defence. Over him Sayer, as my wife, wielded a great hooked scabbard, the classic weaponry of decapitation. Beard (as yours truly), stood at the ready with a vacuum cleaner to, once the head was removed, hoover him out.

Amid the audience's onslaught of hisses and boos and jeers and raspberries – not of the fruity variety, but the sort created from flatulent lingual vibrations – I struggled to comprehend what I was seeing: a bit of light fun? A cheeky supposition? Or an actual indictment, posed graphically for all to see? But then the stage lights dimmed. All went quiet. From the wings appeared Jerome, wheeling out a papier-mâché guillotine with *ACT TWO* flashing upon his head-screen.

My god. I had to flee.

So I fled, my robes billowing like sails.

Sayer had turned Tubbing against me! I had to find my wife. Where might she be? Loitering amid the topiary – no. Moonbathing on the lawn – no luck there, either. I searched far (the horizon) and wide (the other horizon), high and low (literally: up trees, into holes), within the huts and behind the latrines, under every bush and between, optimistically, each blade of grass. Yet there was no sign of her anywhere, or at least not within the boundaries of the Retreat. Which left only one other place: everywhere else.

From the top of the hill I surveyed the jungle all around, which in the moonlight looked as silver and shaggy as the unshorn crotch of an elderly bohemian, and no less moist. As appealing as that might sound, I hesitated. If the buggy abominations of the day 'jigged my timbers,' then their nocturnal counterparts, wriggling and slithering through the dark with their thousand phosphorescent eyes, were literally the stuff of nightmares – specifically *my* nightmares, except now I wore robes instead of the orphanage's belted singlet, and there was no chorus of schoolboys degrading me with rhyming taunts.

Yet find my wife I must, I thought. Find her … then escape!

So summoning all my courage I streamed down the path through the huts and plunged into that putrid, dark heart of vines and creepers and leafy, thorny greens. Almost no light penetrated the canopy. I blundered along through the gloom, hands out to brace any collision with, say, a great spiderweb strung between two trees, which would snag and hold me fast until some dog-sized arachnid came scuttling forth to 'have me.'

It was like falling, that tumble through the jungle's dank inner night. Or more so like drowning in charcoal soup, what with the humidity dampening the air in a tepid mist. As I scurried along, from deep in the trees echoed eerie hoots and cackles – ridicule, perhaps, or simply the jargon of creatures without access to a formal lexicon, and for whom wordless vocalizations were all they could muster to stave off the horror of the void. Who could say what they meant? Not I. I was busy running for my life. And my wife's life, too.

Onward I flailed, as lost and dithering as a bee in the outer reaches of the cosmos. Imagine its confused, intergalactic floundering: this was like that, but instead of dodging comets and meteorites, and having my thorax implode for lack of delicious nectar, my concerns were critters, varmints, predators, divots, tripwires, mildew, wormholes to other dimensions, not to mention a banister of human necks, or a weird man with a rake, or a weird woman with a rake, or some sort of massive, gangly jungle monster with teeth made of hands and salacious yellow eyes where its nipples should be.

And then, suddenly, just as I was about to give up hope: the jungle canopy opened – I was free! And back at the beach where we'd made our arrival. I fell to my knees at the reedy edge of the sands and gazed at the sea: black, boundless, with a silvery stripe painted down its middle by a leering, gibbous moon. The limits of my scheme clarified: I'd not considered, even if I was able to reunite with my wife, how we might abscond to some safer harbour. We had no boat, no chopper, no plane. I was no swimmer; I could barely bathe without thrashing about the tub in an aquaphobic panic.

Despair seized me. My wife would know what to do – but the beach was empty; she was nowhere to be found. Once again, I was alone. Hopelessly, helplessly alone!

But wait.

Something stirred in the waves. I squinted. It looked at first glimpse like an upturned, oversized surfboard: a long plank with bulbous protrusions at either end. But then, as the flotsam drifted into the moonlight those globular shapes revealed themselves as, in fact, human heads. Attached to bodies? Or was this simply the detritus from the guillotine's most recent work – perhaps the cranial remains of the last hapless couple to be condemned as murderers at the Retreat, cast out to sea and a watery grave?

Whatever it was washed shoreward, cresting a wave and then dipping down into the gully, out of sight, before rearing up again. Closer, ever closer, until the mysterious refuse swept upon the beach. Not just heads, bodies trailed behind: two people grasping a single blade detached from a helicopter's main rotor. And now they were moving, crawling out of the surf, abandoning the wreckage that had buoyed them from, I realized, their crash site several miles offshore.

A woman. And a man.

On their knees in the sand. Spent. Exhausted. Barely alive, but certainly in the flesh.

The real Dr. and Mr. Dhaliwal.

Having somehow survived that aerial explosion and plummet to the sea floor, they'd risen like waterlogged phoenixes and now, days later, finally washed up here to claim their rightful places at the Retreat.

Five

There are few occasions in one's life when crisis mutates into advantage. For example, if one's right leg is gnawed off by a gibbon, rarely does the catastrophic loss of limb and mobility become a welcome opportunity to really get to know the left; generally the best one can do is affix a noble peg and clop about town.

As such, you can imagine my horror as the real Dr. and Mr. Dhaliwal came crawling out of the sea like some eight-limbed organism birthed from the primordial muck. Lifting to its many hands and knees, staggering to its four feet, dripping seawater, trailing seaweed, evolving, sneezing (from the salt, I expect), and gazing around with the stupefaction attendant to survival of any sort, maritime or hammock.

My god, I thought; the gig – jig? – was up. The roosters had come home to herald the dawn of truth. The sheep were in the barn, the cows were up a tree, the fish were flopping about with hooks in their eyes, the goats were mauling a farmer for sport, and the imposters were about to be unmasked.

Here were the Dhaliwals in the real, soaking flesh. And what was I? A weird man skulking amid beachfront scrub; a man without a name. A fugitive. A suspect. An accomplice. By proxy, a murderer. And the 'justice of dessert' was about to be served to me in the form of the ice-cold blade of the guillotine, topped with a froth of spinal fluid and plasma and the cherry of my uvula lolling from the top of my gaping neck.

But that, it turned out, was not necessarily the case.

– Where are we? said the real Dr. Dhaliwal, her voice rasping and choked.

– What is 'we'? asked her husband, the true version of me.

– We? Is … Us. No?

– No idea. Can't remember anything.

– Yes. Same.

– What happened?

– I recall –

– A sound.

– A crash?

– A crash. A roar. Water.

– And then?

– I don't know. More water? I –

– Who is 'I'? You?

– I am I, yes. You are ... You.

– My name is You. And yours is I?

– Yes.

– Do you, i.e. I, know ... me, i.e. You?

– I do, I think. You seem familiar. Do You know me?

– 'Me' as in I, as in you?

– Yes?

– Vaguely. Yes.

– Do we have names beyond I and You?

– None that I, as in You, can recall.

Interesting! A scheme began to formulate, gathering heft and momentum like a fearsome sphere of snow tumbling down a mountainside, inhaling the flattened, frozen, amnesiac dead as it went. I began to assemble supplies – vines, mainly, and leaves.

– I am scared.

– I, being You, is also, similarly, scared.

Excellent. A perfect moment to strike. I emerged from hiding, a one-man welcoming committee, my arms spread like the wings of an especially hospitable vampire bat.

– Greetings, I hollered. I am Mr. Dhaliwal. Welcome to the Retreat.

– Oh, hello, said the real Mr. Dhaliwal.

– Hi, said his wife, the actual good albeit forgetful doctor.

– I and You, is it? I asked, approaching steadily.

– I think so, said the man who knew himself only as I.

– Yes, said You. Apparently.

– Wonderful! We've been expecting you – both of you, that is: You and I. Now, please, if you'll allow me to tether your wrists with these vines ... And blindfold you with these leaves ... There we are. And now, if I may lead you along this path, back to the Retreat, where some fine if misguided people will be most intrigued to make your acquaintance, which I'm confident will force them to reconsider some of their previous, ill-considered presumptions about accurately applied justice, when clearly I've arrested – or, rather, *received* the key figures in question. Yes?

– Yes, I think?

– I, as in You, think so too, said the wife. But why must we be bound and sightless?

– Simply a precaution to ensure your safe delivery. It allows me not to lose you in the deep dark woods, or jungle, as you'll see – or not see, rather. As an expert in this terrain, I'll ensure that no monster makes off with you, or that you don't errantly stray into the den of said monster, which will eat your feet.

– Ah, said You. And the blindfolds?

– A fine question, to which I expound: What you don't see, I, can't hurt you, or You.

– I see, replied her husband.

– You don't, that's the point, I clarified. Now! Shall we head off to the Retreat? Please follow me, Mr. I and Mrs. You.

– EYE AND EWE? misheard Jerome. REGARDS, JEROME.

No matter.

– Indeed, I said, nodding at my captives bound and kneeling outside the Welcome Centre, with the starlight – of retribution! – sprinkling upon us from above.

– YOU CLAIM THESE TWO RESPONSIBLE FOR THE MURDER OF … THE VICTIM? REGARDS, JEROME.

– Precisely, I confirmed. I apprehended them attempting to flee by sea. Hence their appearance and overall wetness. 'The proof is made of pudding,' Jerome.

– But, began Mr. Eye.

– And, protested Mrs. Ewe.

– Hush, I cried, snapping their tether like a bullwhip. Vile murderers!

– Whom have we murdered? whimpered Eye.

– Quiet, ghoul. You know exactly whom – don't they, Jerome?

– CERTAINLY IT'S DOWN TO ONE OF TWO NAMES. REGARDS, JEROME.

I lorded over these deadly, sodden assassins in all my glory. Ghouls indeed! What gall to try to swim to freedom after vacuuming the life from arguably the most adored resident of the Retreat – cruelly leaving behind not only a limp epidermal casing, but a skin-caped and blubbering widower, the equally beloved Tubbing.

– So what now, Jerome? I asked. How shall justice be served?

– WITH, OF COURSE, A TRIAL. REGARDS, JEROME.

– A … trial? But they're guilty! I caught them. Clearly they're interlopers here – invaders, even. They reek of fish and treachery. They're not even wearing wristbands!

– A FINE OPENING ARGUMENT FOR YOUR PROSECUTION. REGARDS, JEROME.

– My … Beg your pardon?

– PER THE CONSTITUTION OF THE RETREAT, THE ACCUSED DEFEND THEMSELVES AGAINST THEIR ACCUSER. REGARDS, JEROME.

– Which would be me?

– Me? said Eye.

– Not you.

– Me? said Ewe.

I repositioned the leaf-blindfolds as gags.

– Mrgh, protested Eye.

– Blfq, complained Ewe.

Jerome's head-screen lit up with digital scales. I watched them tip to one side and the other: *Guilty … not guilty. Justice … injustice. Freedom … beheading. Truth … deceit.*

– THE ACCUSED WILL BE DETAINED, said Jerome, WHILE YOU, MR. DHALI-WAL, PREPARE YOUR CASE. JEROME WILL SUBPOENA WITNESSES. REGARDS, JEROME.

– Witnesses?

– YOUR EX-WIFE, FOR EXAMPLE. REGARDS, JEROME.

– Do you mean my *current* wife?

– HOWEVER YOU'D LIKE TO CHARACTERIZE YOUR ESTRANGED MARRIAGE IS FINE. REGARDS, JEROME.

I ventured something daring: – And what of any other suspects? I assume, with these dastards in hand, they would be now absolved? As, for example, my wife, the obviously innocent Dr. Dhaliwal.

– Gwft? said Ewe, suddenly piqued – as if the mention of her real name might have unearthed some buried memory.

– Quiet, you, I scolded, and lashed her tethers like reins. You, Ewe, are no doctor but merely a castaway and murderous knave.

Meanwhile, Jerome's head-screen blinked. He seemed to be searching some sort of database. Or buying time. Finally he spoke:

– DR. DHALIWAL HAS UNWISELY REMOVED HER WRISTBAND. AS SUCH, SHE IS NO LONGER AN OFFICIAL GUEST OF THIS RETREAT. REGARDS, JEROME.

I had no time to comprehend this – my wife was 'persona-non-gratiné'? – for Jerome shot out a grappling hook and seized the accused couple by the leash. Then Eye, Ewe, and I were on the move, herded into the Welcome Centre – down a hall, up an escalator, around a bend, through a gate, etc., until we arrived at a modest door with a piece of paper tacked to it and a single word misspelled thereon: *Liberarry*.

– JEROME TRUSTS THAT THIS WILL PROVIDE A COMFORTABLE AND STIMULATING SPACE TO FORMULATE YOUR CASE AGAINST THE ACCUSED, MR. EYE AND MRS. EWE, FOR THE BRUTAL, SENSELESS MURDER OF ... THE DECEASED. REGARDS, JEROME.

His tray slid out. Upon it was a legal ledger, a fountain pen, and a banana.

– FOR POTASSIUM, said Jerome. REGARDS, JEROME.

With that I was ushered into my provisional office, the door closed behind me, and Jerome led the accused – nay, the killers, the criminals, the contemptible assassins! – away, their footsteps thudding off down the hallway, leaving me to my solitary, stunned, apparently litigious silence.

There were no books in this library, I noticed immediately. Two parallel shelves of videos ringed the room, and in the middle was a writing desk puddled with urine-coloured lamplight, and a chair. I eyed this setup warily, the meagre tools of my summons clutched in my fists. I set the pen and ledger down on the desk, peeled the banana and, to clear my mind, perused the shelves.

The films were in no discernible order, though they included:

Operation Heartstopper

A Fortnight's Caress

The Singe

Strikeforce 5: Armageddon O'clock

On Crepe Mountain

Too Cute to Fail

Attack of the Daddies

The Bungler

Another Grand Hankering

Spare Me Your Dreams

Dryly Through the Poplars, Sharon

Fluffrunner

Dragondancer VII: Sceptre of Eons

Flailing Janet

What a Picnic

Quel Dommage

Live in Concert: Lil Slippy Dingdong & Friends

A Swim to Forget

K.K. Fortune is … the Tower of Knots

A Jeff Among the Kevins

The Slurping Giant Rides Again

Death Legacy 2

The Brownest Rug

Vishwakarma's Wish

Vishwakarma's Regret

The Puma's Kiss

Day of the Morons

Best Barges of the Upper Peninsula

Gregory or Gregor

Before the Hail

Maybe it's My Baby

Writing Your Will: Why Not

Suede for Days

The Vegetarian's Niece

The Septuagenarian's Dad

The Stenographer's Wet Nurse

The Cosmonaut's Ex-Wife and Their Pets

The Celery Farmer's Six Hundred Cousins

The Aesthetician's Attaché

The Department Chair's Hangover

The Fiancée's New Girlfriend in Soweto

The Manservant's Manservant

The Space Bandit's Broker

The Podiatrist's Lovesong

The Podiatrists' Lovesongs

The Submarine Captain's Buddy, Allan

The Gun Runner's Idiot Nephew

The Bootlegger's Imaginary Car

The Invisible Woman's Annoyingly
Visible Hat

The Regrettable Barber's Smell

The Archaeologist's Favourite Trowel

The Eschatologist's Neighbour Who
Whines

The Philanthropist's Mommy

Tristesse, or the Flatware of Paradise

Porcupine Junction (Director's Cut)

Behind the Boring Estuary

Bro, Where's My Arm?!

Gulliver and Happ's Adequate Scheme

163789340123855463872616790541648

Four Days in Whatever

Lil Slippy Dingdong: Alibis and
Lullabies

Brad Beard ... On Wine

Brad Beard ... On Cheese & Wine

Brad Beard ... On Gender

Brad Beard ... On Hope

Brad Beard ... On Funicular Safety

Brad Beard ... On You

Brad Beard ... On Himself

Brad Beard ... On Investment

Brad Beard ... On Cocaine

Brad Beard ... On White-Collar Crime

Brad Beard ... On Prison

Brad Beard ... On Parole

Brad Beard ... On Rebranding

Brad Beard ... On Beards

Brad Beard ... On Beards II

Handsome Janice

Help I'm a Skunk Now

Destiny Rangers: Origins

Murkyman

Spooning Dr. Petrovič

Isle of Slaw

Riches of Fate: The Lil Slippy Dingdong Story

She's Really Got It Out for Derek

The Windy Masseur (Boxset)

Our Gang's Got Gangrene

All Cats on Deck

Waltz of the Janitors

Battlefield Deathcamp III

A Kiss to Try For

Advantage You: Tennis Tips with Gigli
Putnam

Elderly is the Night

G.U.N.K.

Fine, Then

Cereal at Noon

Powerbar Blowout

Holes for Beginners 1 (Your Spade and
You)

Holes for Beginners 2 (Stab, Lift &
Hurl)

Holes for Beginners 3 (Filling it In)

A Flogging of Wimps

Grandma's Lips

Une Vraie Salade
The Great Subterranean Mule Heist
The Dingus
A Lil Slippy Dingdong Christmas
Cry Me a River, Yell Me a Lake
Lobsters vs. Werewolves 2
Ne'er E'en O'er
Prof. L. Sayer Presents: Stroke, Thusly,
   Yes
Scorpion Tidal Wave 2
The Dusk of the Gigolos
Adventures in Fainting
Hangin' With Amber
Mangrove Half-Pipe Xtreme
A Succulence of Cashews
At the Meekest Dawn
Ninja Blood Viper Kill Master Redux
Abigail Sweetgrove: Au Pair Unleashed
Samurai Sous-Chef
Geriatric Psychiatry College Massacre 2
A Shed for Leslie Biederman
Apothecary of Malice
Wacky Raj
Thongworld 4
Jazz Up Your Butt: The 8-Minute
   Workout

Ghost Moat
Demon Moat
Moat of the Damned
The Damnedest Moat
Moat of Fiends
You Say Hiccup; I, Correctly, Say
   Hiccough
Pecorino, Scampare!
Once Bitten, Etc.
Mike's Magic Shoes
The Human Skintag
A Hurricane of Bones
Triplet Fever (Seasons 1–8)
Svetlana the Cuddler
A Vampire's Weirdest Shirt
Worst Mom Ever
The Petulant Ox
Wow, That Was One Druggy Summer
Return to Motel Abdul
Linda's Scent
Linda's Scent, Too
Linda's Scent 3D
Dr. Slipper T. Dingdong, PhD: Who's
   Lil Now
McGraw

The typical titles.

This task exhausted, my banana bitterly vanquished (i.e., peel and all),
I returned to the desk and stood over it, gazing upon that empty ledger.
So this is where I was to condemn Mr. Eye and Mrs. Ewe to their decapitated fates. Or were there less lethal punishments? I brightened, considering: perhaps a rap on the knuckles and a stern scolding from Jerome –
not regards but rebukes. Perhaps the venerable (and venereal) Professor
Sayer would be summoned to perform restorative therapies: off the robes

would come, and out she'd extract their penitence via fondling. Perhaps Tubbing would be called upon per some guilt-inducing sentence, such as an afternoon together in the hammocks or jacuzzi, in which the murderers would be assigned to witness, tolerate, and, where possible, mitigate his ceaseless exhibitions of grief.

With this in mind, I sat. No one need suffer capital or even corporal punishment. Wasn't one cadaver enough? Did we really need three to dispose of? Think of the flies! This is what I'd argue for, I decided: I would be a merciful prosecutor, though the justice I meted would still be as sweet and cold as a frozen shank of sugar cane laced with razor blades: the justice of shame. The most punitive justice of all.

And so I began to write.

When at last I emerged from the library, daylight had arrived. I was exhausted, having scrawled some fifty pages of my typically frantic cursive – penmanship the orphanage's head teacher had once compared to the etchings of a rabid mule into whose hooves someone had wedged a biro. (To which I counter: Would a mule adorn its i's with small hearts? Unlikely.)

I scurried through those hallways, doing my best to recall the route we'd followed from the entrance. But the place remained as mystifying as ever, and each twist and turn from one narrow corridor – carpeted rattily, lit with buzzing fluorescents – to the next only rendered me more lost. Around and around I went, before finally arriving at a dead end with a trap door. Left with no other choice, I entered it and descended – hand over hand, my notepad in my teeth – via ladder to a service level with the infrared lighting of a darkroom. The floors were iron slats, through which I could glimpse the shadowy recesses of another level below – a basement, or sub-basement, or cellar, or the godforsaken dungeon where Brad Beard caged his demons.

The sounds here were a faint metallic hammering, a gasp of passing gasses, the rattle and clang of the pipes, and, finally, a puzzling 'cuckoo.' Fearing I'd instigated an avian mating ritual – was that the thrum of some cocksure display, a gurgle of birdy arousal? – I strode between humidifiers and dehumidifiers and sundry other industrial-grade appliances until I spied a door ahead, light bleeding from the cracks. Though just as I was gathering myself for a final push, another cuckoo sounded right by my ear, followed by a needle-like peck at the lobe – I flung myself forward and slammed through into the adjoining room.

And found myself, appallingly, in some sort of basement aviary.

A thousand sloped, feathery heads swivelled my way. I froze under the piercing, judgmental, and deeply vapid stare of all those glittering, pebble-like eyes. The only sound was the faint hiss of an unseen air vent. The smell was of duvets, but also of fear (my own) and of guano (ideally not my own). The birds roosted uncaged, silently watching me. I'd never seen such a massive, menacing flock. Beaked and winged and demonic.

What fowl hell was this?

Perched around the room were ducks, loons, crows, ravens, finches, tits, boobies, mynahs, eagles, ospreys, hawks, sparrows, wrens, larks, parrots, parakeets, a pair of Siamese pigeons (joined at the wingtip), pigeon-toed hawks, hawk-eyed plovers, cloven-clawed cluckers, a lone two-tufted wingnut, dicky-faced croots, blue-black horners, a scrumph, a hopping cripe, a needle-nosed plier, two canoodling lovebirds, an echo of garbling strappers, a ballad of maroon groovers, a sockhop of tittering jergens, some unbeaked quails, a blockfisted talkie, a meandering strew, a box of dog canaries, a great big tromp, a half-gallon of western misers, a red-feathered bluebird, some pinkish slouses, a slurp-billed ostrigan, and a single, arrogant chicken, or hen, which lorded above all on a shaft of rebar up in the rafters with the despotic, haughty bearing of a Boss.

Observing me thusly, she clucked – once. A cluck of warning. An ominous cluck. A clucky omen: *Proceed not, for we are real peckers.*

For now none of her minions stirred. The room felt as seized as a broken heart.

What to do?

On the far side of the room, at the end of an open path through that eye-plucking gauntlet, which ranged from the predatory to the delicious, I spied a door marked eponymously and hopefully: *EXEUNT.* Some thirty metres away. Would mincing suffice to reach it? Or would my vigilant, timid steps only rile that avian horde to rise as one rapacious, flapping mass and, per the dictate of their clucking master, fall upon me in a threshing of beaks and talons, and gnaw and claw me to death?

Birds! Who knew their tiny, wormy minds?

I tiptoed forward. Silence and stillness reigned. The birds watched. Their Boss blinked once, slowly. Was this permission? Or a stark and final warning? I paused again. Perhaps an introductory address was in order. Some diplomacy. After all, I'd trespassed here without invitation. So, like any responsible ambassador, I curtsied and began.

– Good evening. My name is, unequivocally, Mr. Dhaliwal. As you can see from my wristband, I am a certified lodger at the Retreat, along with my wife, the brilliant if enigmatic Dr. Dhaliwal. I apologize for barging in. I wish only to pass through your habitat, and will, per that classic outdoorsperson's chestnut, take only memories and leave only footprints in your droppings, which, I notice, lacquer the floor most impressively.

I paused. Amid this lavish tapestry of oration, I'd lost the thread. And the Boss was regarding me even more ominously – one eye closed, head 'cocked' – in an appraisal of, I feared, edibility. Devoured by a chicken and her acolytes! It was no way to go. My speech needed more chutzpah, more oomph; I needed not just to 'escape with the hair of my teeth' but to wow and awe and ultimately conquer my audience with the power of rhetoric. I closed my eyes and dug deep within myself, past the pits of despair and fonts of self-flagellation, beyond the vast reservoirs of ruination and lack to that buried trove of ego, worth, freedom, power – that forgotten, untapped wellspring of pride that gurgles secreted and dormant within us all.

I needed to tap my Trunity – in order, as the maxim went, to quite literally pass through to *the other side*.

I needed to unleash my inner Brad Beard.

– Birds, I began, straightening into a more rugged stance: legs splayed, hands on hips, chin high, eyes wide, nostrils flared as if scenting for meat, pelvis prevalent, knees just-so, toes splayed, fingers straight as skate-blades, fingernails neatly trimmed, elbows polished to a glassy sheen, lips juicy, etc.

– Birds, I continued. Birds! You … are birds.

Nodding, I sensed, rippled around the room.

– You are birds, and I am a man. You soar! I crawl, but also walk, and run, and jump. And I can soar, too, in a glider or plane – so there. You caw and warble and squawk, and ostensibly sing, albeit wordlessly and with complete ignorance for verse-chorus-bridge structure. Whereas I discourse and descant, such as this. You eat worms. I … do not, customarily. Why? My greatness lies here.

I tapped my temple, indicating the cerebral circuitry within. But then I spread my arms to encompass my entire body in all its bipedal splendour.

– Think about it: you hatch from eggs – that brittle, obstetric Tupperware – whereas I and my ilk are wrenched shrieking from our mothers' midsections, slick with gore. From the first day of a new baby's life, it has prehensile digits, and a brain to wiggle them. You have – what? Claws? Try fondling a party balloon with those; the results would be mayhem. When the winter comes, humankind does not flee in a disgraceful show of cowardice to warmer climes. We don our snowsuits and tumble joyously into the frost, and from the fallen snow we roll and stack balls into effigies in our own image, which we garnish with probosces of carrot and/or corn – things your kind would heedlessly devour, failing to recognize their aesthetic worth. Pumpkins, same.

Here I paused, sensing some skepticism from a macaw in the back – a flutter of tailfeathers, subdued cooing. Fearing a contaminant 'bird flu' of cheek and disrespect, I barrelled ahead, wielding language as the vaccine with which to cream them.

– *He's for the birds*, we say to dismiss some clueless goof's efforts as foolish or futile. *Bird-brained* is no great compliment either, suggesting an intellect capable of little more than slapping a cheap nest together from twigs and spit. *A bird in the hand … something something*, proceeds another adage, suggesting how easily one might smuggle a fistful of robins into the plumage markets of the northwest. From *going cold turkey*, i.e., plucking oneself hairless for the holiday season, to *cooking one's goose*, cf. tartare, your species has loaned names to all the more disgraceful acts of human endeavour.

– Pieces of eight! protested some parrot vainly.

I ignored this, my gaze fixed on that lofty chicken, or hen. If I could prove myself the alpha, the whole swarm would be mine: it was the rule of the Animal Kingdom and I was nothing if not a wild, rampaging beast. Yet the Boss was stalwart and returned an unwavering stare of her own, haughty and powerful. And, my god, even as I watched she sat up to puff-and-fluff, as if prepping a rebuttal (or to lay an egg, who could say?).

My finale would need to be virtuosic.

– Some say that birds are the last vestiges of the dinosaurs. What a sorry end befell those losers, and out you folks slithered from the meteor-hole. And then what? Eons of flapping about the sky, gulping bugs, while humankind evolved with patience, toward perfection, and then toiled upon the earth to build the very structures upon which you would so flagrantly, ubiquitously defecate: the pyramids, the skyscrapers, the bridges and the bus stops. To what end? I submit: this one, here now. The cluck stops here.

I paused, letting this linguistic wizardry sink in.

– And so, submit to me, my feathered friends. Know your true master. Let me pass unmolested. No pecking, no swooping. I don't want to hear so much as an errant caw. And once I am gone from here, you may tell your offspring of the day a human dignified your lair, and how the wisdom he imparted left you feeling not invaded, disrupted, or disturbed, but enervated, enlightened – and grateful. For the words he spoke, viz. the words I'm speaking now, revealed the hierarchy of beings: humans at the top, and every other creature heaped subordinately below. And that is what Trunity means to me.

It was over. I bowed. Yet my lecture garnered no applause, only more portentous silence. Were they simply mesmerized? No: from their roosts the birds stared at me, unmoving – and seemingly unmoved.

With dread I looked up to the rafters. The Boss was up on her back legs now, wings splaying, wattle catching the breeze like a windsock. And then she was on the move – lifting off, coasting down, almost elegant, were it not for the look of profound vacuity in her eyes and the sumptuous heft of her breast. I flinched as she neared, closing my eyes – she would not take them so easily. But amid a whooshing of air about my face I felt a weight settle upon my head, a little scuttle of claws, and then stillness. And warmth.

I opened my eyes. The chicken, or hen, had alighted upon my head. And now rested there peacefully in the manner of a hat.

At this the other birds sprung to life: the room resounded with a great cacophony of hoots, chirps, whistles, shrieks, peeps, whippoorwilling, tittering, twittering, chittering, chattering, cawing, crowing, warbles, chirrups, an anomalous moo, a yawn, screes, honks, quacks, coos, and so forth, while heads bobbed and wings flapped and birdy bodies hopped from one foot to another in a dance of something like glee.

My god. They were laughing at me.

Regardless its oomph and valour, my speech had accomplished nothing. Perhaps the opposite. In one literal fell swoop the Boss had trumped me and proved the victor. I could pass through her domain, but only if I wore her like a crown of thorns – or poultry. And so, with the forlorn, sheepish gait off the trounced, I performed my walk of defeat through the chortling avian masses, toward the door, *EXEUNT*, and through it, to whatever awaited me and my passenger on – yes – *the other side.*

Six

After a fitful, restless nap – if you've ever tried to bed down with a bird on your head you'll appreciate my struggles – I rose feeling groggy and wary, not to mention befeathered. Certainly, I'd crafted a rhetorically impeccable legal argument proving the unequivocal guilt of the interlopers Eye and Ewe, ergo absolving me and my wife of any wrongdoing. Yet I'd also failed to convince a roomful of birds that I was their better, and had been punished with the fowl burden of that failure.

I missed my wife, who was still missing. And now that we were in the clear, I needed to send her an update: a bottled message hurled into the surf, a facsimile transmission cabled screaming across telephonic lines. All was well! Or would be. Even if she had forgone her status at the Retreat, I remained the Mr. to her Dr. and would shortly defend her honour in court by incriminating two strangers. Wasn't this what marriage was all about? Loyalty, trickery, absolution?

Forgoing breakfast, my feathery passenger and I spent the morning again searching the compound. With everyone firmly and greedily ensconced in the Dining Hall, ravaging metre-tall stacks of pancakes and great jaundiced knolls of egg, I traced a route through the huts, poking my head inquisitively into each one. I was amazed at their uniformity, yet each domicile also struck me with the uncanniness of a dreamspace: while the details were consistent – bunks, dresser, pornography-streaming TV – they all seemed skewed in some inarticulable way. And then there was Tubbing's hut, with its chalk outline upon the doorstep, which I inadvertently scuffed and had to nudge back into shape; the result looked like a tumour blooming from the dead man's back.

– Bock, scolded the Boss from atop my cranium.

On I scurried, around the Welcome Centre to locales beyond. I checked behind and within dumpsters, in a little shed that housed gardening tools and the huts where the pool's filtration system growled like some grumpily slumbering beast. I peered into the pool itself, ensuring my wife wasn't simply resting upon its floor in an iron lung (she was not), and, at the hot tub, rolled up my sleeve to grope around that great frothing soup for her form – no luck either. The hammocks were likewise empty, as was an area equipped with what I first took to be an assortment of torture devices, but which upon closer inspection appeared to comprise the weight-lifting apparatuses of a 'Jim.'

My search exhausted, I sat upon a sawed-off stump by the trailhead. As the Boss preened and mewled softly, I took stock of what I knew and what I did not.

Fact, seemingly: Dr. Dhaliwal was neither hiding upon the grounds of the Retreat nor on the beach, nor on the path thereto.

Supposition: it seemed unlikely that she would be holed up somewhere inside the Welcome Centre, which Jerome patrolled day and night.

Near impossibility: she'd 'gone to sea.' She'd told me to wait. She'd promised she'd be back. And besides, as Tubs and Pudding had confirmed, there was no way off the island.

If I knew my wife at all – and, again, I didn't really – there was only once place she might have gone: down that sawdust path, into the trees … and back to the village. To the tower beyond the market, that strange chapel and its slumped parishioners. But why? To harness them as an army? I pictured Dr. Dhaliwal, sporting the telltale beret of the jungle commandant, training that silent congregation in guerrilla warfare – winnowing through the underbrush, spears in their teeth, fingernails sharpened to bayonets.

Despite the blasting sunlight, I shivered. The path was only a few steps away, and the village a short walk beyond that. If I could retrieve my wife it would be a simple negotiation to still her armed insurrection: through the power of language and the rule of law – and deceit – I had built a watertight, watershed case. Come back, I would say, sweet darling; there's nothing to fear or fight.

I rose from my stump with rekindled passion and purpose. Even the Boss, cooing her encouragement, seemed primed for a rescue mission.

But then a roar sounded behind me. I turned to discover a great mob surging from the back doors of the Welcome Centre. Brad Beard, Professor Sayer, Jerome, Tubbing (curiously arm-in-arm with those two women in the hand-painted beards), and every last Retreater, thrashing toward me in a conflagration of hooting, hollering, and facial hair. Grinning wildly. Cresting the little rise between the swimming pool and hot tub and tumbling down the path, a mass of hysterical derangement, eyes wide and delirious –

Coming for yours truly.

I had no time to move. That roiling, delirious crowd fell upon me like a siege of locusts. I felt myself seized by the ankles and wrists. Hands found my calves, my thighs, my back, my shoulders – my buttocks! – and lifted me off the ground, over their heads. This was too much for the Boss: she took to the wing and flapped away. The sun, that great white eye, glared down as if through a spyhole in the sky as I was jostled and bounced, and my pallbearers' jumbled shouts coalesced into a musical refrain:

– *Mr., Mr. Dhaliwal! / Dolly, Polly, Wally, y'all! / Missed their sister; what's his name?*

So this is how it would end: carted by a rampaging, chanting mob to the guillotine, and then beheaded as they cavorted about to inanely corrupted limericks. Clearly Eye and Ewe had regained their memory and 'thrown a bus atop me.' The truth was out. And everyone was singing it. And, my god, here came another verse!

– *Mr., Mr. Dhaliwal! / Falls a jolly folly ball! / Whisper 'whisker'; what's his name?*

We were on the move now. I felt hands groping me, everywhere – not entirely unpleasurable, yet I ignored the titillation to contemplate my mortality. Had I lived a 'good life'? What might that entail? Amid his gory probings, I'd never seized and kissed my dentist full on the lips, for example – an existential regret? Or a triumph of will and moral fortitude?

Yet we weren't, I realized, heading through the jungle to the waiting blade. Instead I was conveyed back up the hill to the Welcome Centre. I squirmed to get a better view, but hands firmly forced my face to the heavens, per whatever solar ritual heralded my sacrifice. Though perhaps

I was not heading to slaughter, but in fact being feted? Their meaning was hard to parse, but the chants did seem to suggest a tone of celebration:

   – *Mr., Mr.. Dhaliwal! / A ballsy collie smally galls. / Frisk her brisker; what's his name?*

We pushed through the doors and inside. Considerately, to avoid my face being smeared along the ceilings, I was lowered to shoulder-height, my vision swimming greenly as it adjusted to the fluorescents of the Welcome Centre hallways. Vaguely I could make out the faces surrounding me: beaming, feverish, ecstatic. Was this Tubbing, clutching my left elbow? Yes: his skin-cape waved like a pennant upon patriotic winds.

   – Tubbing, I hissed, where are you taking me?

   – Why, to your Shower! he cried.

My god. Stripped and washed by all these people? I was no profligate nudist. Not to mention the prospect of scouring pads and loofas forcefully exfoliating my most secret and sacred parts. Showered? I'd rather be decapitated, I thought.

   – *Mr., Mr. Dhaliwal! / 'All be,' calls he, 'cauli-flaws.' / Twist her blister; what's his name?*

I closed my eyes as I was ferried through the maze of passageways. Into an elevator, up a floor or two, and then out, ascending a sloping ramp, and finally bursting into what I could only assume was the bathhouse in which I would be stripped and hosed like a contaminated sheep. But to my astonishment I was only lowered gently, fully robed, and found myself in a kind of sitting room: a giant, rectangular pit lined with sofas on all sides, headed by the 'power seat' onto which I'd been placed. And then handcuffed, at the wrist, to the armrests. Trapped! But reverently.

   – *Mr., Mr. Dhaliwal! / 'A palled atoll, a ball o' shawls,' / Hissed her kisser; what's his name?*

Everyone sat. The chants and mania abated. I realized that the chair from which I lorded was a throne – an elaborate, baroque piece of furniture with gilded flames licking from armrests to headrest. The arm-restraints were leather. The cushions: velvet.

Jerome glided forward in a deferential bow. – GREETINGS. REGARDS, JEROME.

   – Hi Jerome, I said.

He wheeled to face the group. – PLEASE GREET: THE ADVOCATE!
REGARDS, JEROME.

The ovation that thundered through the room felt physical, a kind of aural assault. Amid the rollicking crowd I spied Tubbing smooching his artificially bearded lovers. Mid-kiss, over their shoulders, he flashed me an enthusiastic thumbs-up.

Then they were all chanting again:

– *Solicitor, barrister, attorney, counsel … / The Advocate's here to mete the truth! / Murderer, philanderer, reprobate, sinner … / The Advocate will blade you, by hook or by struth!*

What proceeded can only be described as the driest, most indulgent shower I'd ever 'enjoyed': a shower not of water, soapy lather, and poos sham and other, but a kind of grotesque, tempestuous dowry ... A shower of presents!

Jerome loosened my restraints, nodded to acknowledge my freedom, and ordered the ceremony to begin. Here came the first gift, which I unearthed from great frothing irruptions of tissue paper. A cyclone of grins deluged me as I unfurled and displayed the contents: a set of towels (bath, hand, face), each one monogrammed vainly, *Mr. D., Adv.*

– THE ADVOCATE'S TOWELS, announced Jerome. REGARDS, JEROME.

The applause was boisterous and embarrassing.

– Thank you, I said, folded the towels back into their bag, and retreated in my seat, out of the 'light of limes' that inundated me from all sides.

But this was only the beginning. Immediately someone handed me another present, garnished with a great lurid bow, in a gift-wrapped box the size of a microwave oven.

– THE ADVOCATE'S MICROWAVE OVEN, announced Jerome as I grudgingly revealed the thing inside. REGARDS, JEROME.

– Thank you, I said.

This went on: Jerome announced each new bequeathal as I unwrapped and displayed it to the room: a gold watch, some silver spoons, porcelain dinnerware, a dozen wineglasses, half a dozen beer glasses, a pair of sunglasses (from Tubbing, possibly the same pair he'd leant me at the market), teacups, coffee cups, a snooker cue in a velveteen case, a full complement of patio furniture, keys (to a car? a house? a treasure chest? Professor Sayer only bounced her eyebrows suggestively), bed linens, a straitjacket, alpine skis, cross-country skis, water skis, ski goggles, squash goggles/racquet/three-pack of balls, a box (packaged inside an identical if slightly larger box – discarded), a pickaxe, a hand vacuum that Jerome encouraged me to try (it roared and sucked; everyone clapped), *The Complete Works of Brad Beard: Vols. 1–8* (Vols. *9–15*, Mr. Beard elucidated, were available for advance purchase), a chainsaw, a headband, and on and on and on and on, the applause cresting and waning like surf. Meanwhile each successfully opened gift was manoeuvred into a sort of holding area behind my throne; as the haul grew this began to resemble the contents of a sudden estate sale after the town robber baron has unexpectedly perished.

With a final gift – mousetraps – the shower was over and Jerome re-handcuffed me, with a robotic flourish, to my throne. I felt as if someone had tapped me like a maple tree, extruded every last drop of lifeblood from my veins, and forced me to watch as they boiled the gurgling juice into syrup. I withered in my seat. My eyelids and limbs drooped. All around me towered tissue and ribbon and bows and elaborately patterned paper. Yet my audience still beamed at me with those same looks of rapture. Nearly one dozen couples tilted toward me with identical expressions – awe-struck, enamoured, hungry. It felt dubious and unearned. What was I meant to do? Or say? Or be?

– Speech! cried Tubbing, echoed by huzzahs from his two merry wives. This elicited a roar of approval, from which evolved another chant:

– *Speech, speech, speech! / For everyone, each to each. / So open your ears / And quiet your fears / For the Advocate's about to preach.*

At least this verse obeyed some formal prescriptions.

Peering into all those keen, intoxicated faces, I tried to discern what they needed. 'Preach' seemed to imply a sermon, something spiritual to boost their souls to the heavens. I searched for the words to herald this ascension. But nothing came. My disappointing silence stiffened the air. No one so much as blinked. Their unrelenting gaze seemed intent on tugging something essential from me. But whatever I might offer them, I sensed, would only emerge stillborn and failed.

My last attempt at oration had resulted in humiliation-by-chicken. (Or hen.) And now, despite my Shower, I'd never felt so spiritually unclean. Nothing I could say would be enough – never mind that the greatest Speaker of the modern era was only inches away, peering at me from within a beard as lush as a thicket.

The cursor on Jerome's head blinked hungrily, urgently.

– PLEASE, he prompted. FEEL FREE TO BEGIN ANY TIME. REGARDS, JEROME.

– *Speech, speech, speech,* they chanted. *The Advocate's sweet as a peach. / He's a man with a plan / For two freaks on the lam / And their lesson's about to be teached.*

Credit them for trying. I opened my mouth and, unsure what might come out, did my best to tell them what they wanted to hear.

– I am the Advocate, I confessed.

It sufficed. A great cheer rose up; if I'd had anything more to say, the clamour of voices would have drowned it out. But all that bellowing and ululating, that stamping and stomping, that applause, synchronizing now into rhythmic handclaps – like a pulse, like a death-knell – wasn't for me, nor for my rousing opening remarks. These people were celebrating their own benevolence and goodwill, and, ultimately, themselves. No one was even looking at me anymore: they peered around at one another, met eyes in brief compacts of mutual acclaim, then moved on to the next bedfellow in self-congratulations. Grins became smirks; chests puffed outward. *Me!* they seemed to boast. *I'm the one! Me!*

Their fanfare now excluded yours truly. It raged and swelled like a hurricane, surrounding and pressing in and marooning me upon my throne. So I huddled there, wrists pinned to the armrests, as one might shelter under an awning from a rainstorm, peering out into the drizzle.

And then, with some final chirps and tweets, it was over. The silence that followed felt hollow and spent.

I waited.

Jerome rolled forward, his display screen ablaze with icons of fire.

– AND NOW, he announced, ON WE CONTINUE TO THE ADVOCATE'S ROAST! REGARDS, JEROME.

Again I was hoisted onto the shoulders of the revellers and carted through the Welcome Centre (no songs now; just a sort of officious parade) down to the basement and the Conference Room, where they deposited me onstage upon an identical plush-cushioned, high-backed throne, cuffed my wrists to the armrests, and retreated, bowing.

The lights dimmed. A spotlight located and blinded me. Another wiggled around the stage – provocative, almost sultry. Bombastic music heralded the grandiloquent event: my imminent 'Roast,' apparently.

Would I be burned alive? I scanned the floor for kindling. Yet I discovered only a snakelike tangle of cables connecting a lone microphone to speakers flanking the stage. A light electrocution then, perhaps via my wristband? Or might I be roasted by hairdryer cranked to scorching and thrust up my robes? I closed my eyes and steeled myself for the worst. Though no imagined terror could have prophesied what I was about to endure.

The music silenced. I opened my eyes. The spotlight had seized upon the microphone stand and girdled it now in a silvery halo. Hissing sounded from the wings and out coughed clouds of synthetic fog. And then, skipping from behind the curtain with all the jollity of a child unleashed into a margarine factory, came Brad Beard, waving and grandstanding to wild applause as the stage lights flashed red and green and blue – the definitive palette of impending entertainment.

The crowd settled. Brad Beard lorded behind the microphone with his arms raised in a triumphant V – for his own imminent Victory, or the looming Vengeance of the trial … or was he simply commanding his acolytes' Veneration? My god, his beard had really 'gone wild,' sprouting impetuously from his face in flamboyant tufts, while his sunglasses mirrored his audience's worship back to them.

I, meanwhile, trapped upon my throne, beardlessly awaited my fate.

– Friends! he began, at which everyone – even I, despite myself – leaned closer: had we, simply by proximity, become actual chums and confidantes of the Great Man?

No.

He chuckled, shaking his head, as if the mere suggestion of fraternal equity between us, his slavish devotees, and he, our pre-eminent guru, was not just unimaginable, but hilarious. What rhetoric, though! He really had me.

– *Friends*, he continued, with palpable irony, I'm here today, and you're here too, not just to celebrate our beloved the Advocate before his big day in court. We're here, upon the eve of his trial, to roast the living daylights out of him.

I noticed Tubbing stationed front row – in the very seat from which Brad Beard had once plucked and exemplified him. His new wives sat on either side of him, beards smudged up their cheeks, and the entire throuple's eyes flamed with retribution – or the anticipation of it. Tubbing, especially, had the rapacious look of one desperate for validation, for some public and adulated figure to speak to words the voiceless flesh of his ruined heart.

Instead:

– But, first, you should know that copies of the brand-new, revised edition of my first book, *Becoming Beard*, a memoir of sorts, though legally obviously I'm not allowed to call it that, are now available for sale in the Gift Shop.

Tubbing wrapped the cape of his dead husband around himself a little more snugly.

Beard continued:

– While I'm sure all of you have read the original edition multiple times, this version, which is at least partially authorized by yours truly, contains several never-before-seen graphs and pie charts and, I think, some other stuff, including probably some pictures, that will really help maximize your Inner Ventures.

A ruffling of robes; wallets were readied.

– But hold your hats for now, because first I'd like to bring up our host, without whom which we wouldn't even be here, literally, because holy crow, you know? I mean is it amazing in this Welcome Centre or what? As in it's like *a maze*.

Obedient laughter.

– Anyhoo. Friends, please put your hands together for everybody's favourite robot-concierge … the mighty … the cylindrical … *Jerome!*

Brad Beard stepped aside and Jerome glided out from backstage. The fog machines woofed out some nimbostratic puffs. The coloured lights blinked. The applause was wan.

– THANK YOU, ILLUSTRIOUS BRAD BEARD, said Jerome. ROASTERS, PLEASE QUEUE SIDE-STAGE SO WE CAN PROCEED IN AN ORDERLY FASHION. AND, WITHOUT FURTHER ADO, JEROME WILL RETURN THE MICROPHONE TO –

Brad Beard bounded back into the spotlight and nudged Jerome aside. The crowd's rejuvenated hoots and howls drowned out the robot's mannerly sign-off. And for a moment I pitied Jerome, wobbling off into the shadows.

– *Queue?* yelled Beard. What are we, taking turns like a round of patty-cake? What kind of baby's Roast is that? Nope, a Roast is a *Roast*. Raging as a bonfire. No turns, no order. Just a whole lot of roasting and the Advocate soaking it in. So let's go for it, yeah?

He turned the microphone so it faced the audience. A wail of feedback faded into merciful, glorious silence in which nothing happened, and no one said a word, and I just sat there, handcuffed to my throne, begging for that glorious nothingness to bloom and swell until it filled the room and swallowed us all.

But then, of course, they began.

– The Advocate smells like noodles, but worse!

  – I once saw the Advocate eat pucks from a latrine!

  – I saw it too! Then he sneezed in some soup!

  – And ate it! He ate his own sneeze-soup!

  – The Advocate is bad at math!

  – The Advocate is bad at kissing!

  – I kissed the Advocate once and he led with his ears!

  – The Advocate can only count to six and he goes one-two-fourteen-six!

  – Want to confuse the Advocate? Put him in a small boat and push him into the lake. The guy doesn't even know how to row. He thinks you do it with wishing!

  – Knock-knock. Who's there? The Advocate, so out to lunch he missed the doorbell!

  – Ever go out for lunch with the Advocate? Me neither. No one has!

  – No one's ever even seen the Advocate before!

  – Who are we talking about? The Advocate? Never heard of him!

  – I don't even know what I'm yelling about!

  – Down with the Advocate!

  – Up the Advocate's wazoo!

  – Upbraid the Advocate!

  – Braid the Advocate's hair and then cut it all off and put the braids up his nose and make him say, *I'm a stupid walrus, look at me!*

  – You call that a beard, the Advocate? It looks like a face made of skin!

  – I tried to teach him how to grow a beard and he got confused and cuddled a tree!

  – Shall we elucidate the Advocate's recent malfeasance as an artisanal hairbrush manufacturer? First, the dubious materials: handles of black-market ivory and bristles plucked from live porcupines. The goal being, of course, to make his customers feel that their own hairbrushes – modest affairs of plastic and rubber – were inadequate: ergo, they, too, were inadequate. Ever conniving, ever solicitous, the Advocate hawked his wares to these fine people as the salve to all that ailed them. And the result? Tangles. Knots. Tears. The hairbrushes didn't even work! Heads were shaved. Tresses were culled and put out with the trash. And what did the Advocate do? Collected all that hair, stitched it into toupees, and hawked wigs to the shorn and humiliated. The whole hairbrush operation had been a scheme to twice line his pockets! Yet when the local authorities launched an investigation, the fellow skipped town – on to the next grift, no doubt. Typical Advocate: another shameful episode in the life of an utterly shameful man!

– I wish the Advocate's robes were made of itches and spiders!

– I wish the Advocate was dead!

– WERE DEAD. REGARDS, JEROME.

– If the Advocate *were* dead he'd be better than he is now, by which I mean alive!

– Kill the Advocate!

– Let's kill him!

– Yeah, get him, cut off his hands!

– Cut off his unbearded face!

– Let's skin him alive until he's dead! Oh, shoot – sorry, Tubbing. Touchy subject?

– Kind of, yeah.

– Though think about it: he doesn't even have a spouse, and you've got two!

– Three, Tubbing, if you count the dead one!

– Thank you, I will admit that I'm considerably happier now in this throuple with these two lovely, luxuriantly and legitimately bearded ladies!

– Hooray for Tubbing! Nay to the Advocate!

– Neigh! Neigh!

– Hee-haw! Hee-haw!

– Tubbing's got two lovers and the Advocate's got none! Being alone is weird!

– He's a weird lonely freak! The Advocate, I mean!

– The Advocate's a sad divorcé!

– He sleeps in his car and scours the Classifieds for basement apartments!

– If he has a car! He doesn't!

– Every night, after a supper of canned stew and bagged prewashed lettuce that the Advocate eats standing in his darkened kitchenette, he fills a child-sized yellow plastic cup with ice-cold red wine he caps with tinfoil and returns to the crisper before drinking by the light of his fridge wondering how seriously to take the expiry date on his ketchup, totally alone!

– No, the Advocate lives on egg salad sandwiches from a vending machine at the bus station. He eats half before ten and saves the other half for lunch, except by the time he gets it out again at 2:30 it's gone so soggy and depressing that it's become a kind of paste – but he eats it anyway, slurping it off the side of his hand, totally alone!

– Speaking of ketchup, ever see the Advocate *without* mustard on his shirt? Me neither!

– I thought it was egg! From the egg salad sandwiches!

– Mustard!

– Looks like egg though!

– Agree to disagree!

– Does anyone even love the Advocate? I asked around and oh-for-twenty-four, everyone I talked to said nope, not me, no way!

– Nobody loves the Advocate!

– Ha ha, he's going to die alone!

– The Advocate's going to die!

– It's true, the Advocate's totally going to die!

– Indeed, one day the Advocate will die. And what will become of him then?

I emerged from the Roast even more harrowed than I had from the Shower. Yet once I was freed from my throne, the insults turned back into accolades – for my willingness to suffer their abuse without rebuttal or protest, I assume. I slunk out of the Conference Room through this perverse gauntlet of praise, longing for the sanctity of my hut, and hoping, vainly, for the deranged festivities to end.

Yet of course my peril had only begun. I was chased into the hallway by the mob, which accosted and encircled me – teeth bared, as if the next phase of their revelry might involve feasting upon my flesh.

– NEXT, said Jerome, WE MOVE TO THE ADVOCATE'S BANQUET AND HEN-DO. REGARDS, JEROME.

I heard *honeydew*. A rite of melon-eating? That I could stomach. I would have preferred the mighty cantaloupe to the honeydew's sickly verdigris, but anything was better than being lashed to a chair and besieged with insults and lies under the pretence of merriment. Yes, melon! Sliced into wedges, please, to gnaw from the rind.

But then a fluttering sound disturbed my reverie. From the shadows swooped a familiar winged and feathery creature – I ducked, but not before the Boss alit upon my head. Clasping my temples with its talons, the creature crowed triumphantly and resumed its humiliating roost.

Everyone cheered.

THE ADVOCATE'S HEN, narrated Jerome. NOW, HIS BANQUET. REGARDS, JEROME.

And up I was lifted, and off we went – to the Dining Hall.

– *To supper, then his hen-do*, the mob chanted as they carried me. *The Advocate's still ours for a few (hours)! / We'll eat and drink and dance and sing, too. / The Advocate won't be blue. It's true!*

Their worst effort yet. A metrical disaster.

Either my throne had been transported to the Dining Hall or it was another duplicate into which I was once again deposited and shackled. The tables had been organized into one long, banquet-style affair at which everyone took their seats, with Brad Beard commandeering the position at the far end – complicating which of us was the meal's head, and which its asinine posterior – and raised a goblet in salutation.

– I'd like to offer a cheers, before we dine, to the Advocate!

Everyone raised their goblets – except me, what with my wrists strapped to the armrests. Atop my head, the Boss fluffed her feathers and nestled down to sleep; the warmth from her body might have been almost soothing were it not for Brad Beard, whose address turned stentorian.

– What a guy! he roared. From the first time I casted eyes on him I thought, *Okay here's someone.* And am I right or am I right! About the Advocate? All of you no doubt are cognizant with my First Behest of First Impressing: *Dress Your Best to Impress the Rest.* And while that might not be so much relevant here? If anyone knows something or two about *advocacy*, it's, you know … Anyway, to the Advocate! Huzzah!

– *To the Advocate! Huzzah!*

– Thank you, I said.

The Banquet was a strange affair. In pairs the Retreaters were summoned by Jerome to a bucket-sized cauldron steaming on a hot plate at the side of the room. From its depths they scooped out a ladle of whatever goulash or potage simmered therein and approached me with it, whispering:

– *The Advocate must beat the heat, so we entreat the Advocate to eat.*

The ladle was nudged between my lips and obediently I accepted the slop one viscous mouthful at a time. Adrift in a dark, glutinous gravy were sinewy clots of flesh (boar? hedgehog? ibis?) alongside shreds of bread and cheese and fruit and veg, with an aftertaste that suggested the saline tang of the sea. The flavour was neither terrible nor particularly alimental, perhaps best described as 'comprehensive' – as if the whole buffet had been run through the blender, and here was the ghastly conglomerate of everything on offer, served at once.

– Thank you, I said, each time.

Beyond the mantra that accompanied each new turn at the ladle, no one spoke. The only other sounds through my Banquet were the chime of cutlery and the epiglottal gurgle of human swallowing. The absence of discourse was at first welcome, considering the previous bombardments, but, as the meal progressed, it began to feel unnatural – and then discomfiting. I longed for the company of my wife, whose taciturn dialogue would have been welcome amid this tense and delicate silence, which felt less ceremonial than imposed, as if by ordinance or martially enforced decree. What punishment, I wondered, might be in store for anyone who broke it?

As I sat there, grinning graciously as each subsequent couple fed me their ladleful of conglomerated goop, I thought more actively, and desperately, of Dr. Dhaliwal. Those green, scrabbling branches of longing became a yellow mist of yearning, and finally the conflagratory reddish haze of desire. But not some lusty desire, cheap and damp and moaning; no, I simply felt a deep, abiding need to clutch and hold her – hand-to-hand, head-to-head, cheek-to-cheek, eye-to-eye. I recalled our transit here, bodies pressed into that fragile embrace, and envied all these couples for the cuddles they'd later enjoy in their huts. (Tubbing would get it from both sides.)

Then it was over. The stew pot was empty. Jerome cleared the table. All eyes fixed upon me. Atop my cranium, the Boss roused herself, cooed, readjusted, and resumed her nap. I couldn't have moved even were I unfettered from my throne; I must have consumed a quarter of my body weight in stew and felt fairly embalmed by the stuff.

Down at the far end of the table Brad Beard sat back, sipping from his goblet, his lips and teeth and beard stained a brilliant ruby colour. He nodded at me from some fifty feet away – a nod of condescension, I felt, as if he were my host, or guardian, or master.

– Well, the Advocate? Have you enjoyed your Banquet?

– Thank you, I said.

– No, said Brad Beard, thank *you*. With all our gratuity. Right, 'friends'?

Everyone thumped the table with their goblets, then downed the remaining dregs.

– And now, the Advocate?

A dramatic pause before the last thing I would remember from that night:

– Now, said Brad Beard, we treat you to the g-darn Hen-Do of a lifetime.

Session #5 Transcript

– Okay, Mr. Dhaliwal, or, should I say, *the Advocate*, we're rolling, and, no, my intonation there is not meant to sound sardonic or doubtful, but merely to annunciate the importance of your position, as the agent of justice, here, at the Retreat, for which I, for one, am grateful, as are we all, as I hope was made sufficiently clear during yesterday's ceremonies, which, I must apologize, I was mostly unable to attend, post-Roast, about which I will only say, now, that I hope the key that I gifted you, fits, as they say, some appropriately lubricated lock, if you know what I mean.

– Someone filled my head with cement and smashed it with a sledge-hammer.

– A mighty Hen-Do, then, one for the ages, excellent, and, I will add, as a culmination of the day's festivities, one would be hard-pressed to think of a greater tribute to your posterity than inebriation so total, so complete, that you are rendered physically and mentally incompetent for the subsequent twenty-four hours, and, yet, of course, we must continue our work, here, even if it is in the form of a solo Session, as your wife continues to be unaccounted for, and yet you must be commended, Mr. Dhaliwal, the Advocate, for having apprehended two criminals in our midst, or at the periphery of our midst, fleeing, was it, the murder scene, you're really turning things around, and, speaking of, while I am not at liberty, per the oaths of my profession, and their attendant standards of confidentiality, to reveal the content of my Sessions with other patients, I will briefly say that the husband of the deceased, a certain Mr. Tubbing, might have revealed to me, and I quote, 'Were it not for my failed conjoin-ing with the Advocate I never would have found Trunity in this really cool throuple,' and, sorry, Mr. Dhaliwal, let me just check my notes, they're right here, I don't want to misquote the man, considering everything he's been through, and, ah, yes, here we are, 'and probably drowned myself in the hot tub,' and, so, what a testament to your presence, here, at the Retreat, for which we are all grateful, as I hope yesterday's celebrations made clear.

— *Celebrations?*

— Certainly, yes, justice remains to be served, as Mr. Tubbing, has, let's not forget, suffered a loss, and, dare I say, tragedy, which no one should ever experience, even if now at night he might turn for comfort, companionship, and the solace of the flesh, to not just one, but *two* distinct lovers, wow, things are really working out for him in that throuple, about which, incidentally, in my Sessions with him and his lovers, while I shouldn't divulge specific details, among his disclosures, let me check my notes again, yes, here it is, 'Sometimes at night we take the pillows and form them into the shape of a man and cloak that pillow-man in my skin-cape and involve him in our fun,' which, wow, Mr. Dhaliwal, is that not some provocative stuff, our friend Tubbing is certainly on his way, as my colleague Bradley might say, through Trunity, and beyond it, to *the other side*.

— How much longer is this going to be?

— That's precisely it, Mr. Dhaliwal, the existential question we all must consider, one that was introduced, I thought, quite artfully, in yesterday's Roast —

— My god, please. No more roasting.

— Oh, Mr. Dhaliwal, the Advocate, whatever, your posture, now, cowering and eyeing the door, suggests, perhaps ungratefully, that you view the Roast as a torturous experience, when, in fact, to have one's greatness venerated, ironically, with insults, should feel like a testament to said greatness, and I wonder if we might examine your instinct to feel victimized, as well as your physical response, which resembles the shrivel of the potato bug, and which, I believe, speaks to your fundamental misapprehension about certain, shall we say, human interactions, particularly those of physical intimacy, which, if I just slide in beside you, we might begin to challenge, holistically, if you are ready to try?

— Well, no, not really.

– No?

– No. I think that's enough for today, Professor Sayer.

– But, Mr. Dhaliwal, my dear Advocate, we've only just begun –

– Goodbye, Professor Sayer.

– I'm, wait, sorry, do you mean, actually, goodbye?

– Yes. Goodbye.

Seven

In my hut that evening, before bedding down for the night, I revised and rehearsed my opening argument, scripted in a banana-fuelled fervour, for the trial:

– A few words about justice, they, and I, began.

– For what is justice? Something weighed by a Lady blindfolded with a tea towel. Yet the scales of justice are serpentine too: scaly, certainly, though not nearly as slimy as you might think. For justice is a snakelike thing slithering through the weeds, then rearing up in a great cauled theatric of fangs and tongues and venom, yellow-eyed and beady. Not to forget the lyricism of *poetic* justice, those verdicts recited in verse – dactyls, iambs, diphthongs, one-piece thongs, and all. If there's a more elegant way of being condemned to a lifetime of incarceration … Piper, play on!

– What is crime? Breaking the law. And the law? The rules for what not to do, or be, as well as why, where, when and how not to do or be anything, ever. Ignorance of the law is no excuse, they say, which means that all of us should spend a few years reading up on every edict and verdict, ever. It's our responsibility; it's our right. For that's what the law is: rights and responsibilities. Irresponsible leftists need not apply! No, that's simply a humorous joke. Most criminals aren't bad people, simply hooligans and miscreants whose parents failed them, probably at the holidays.

– One hears about the labour of justice and its key, overtaxed employee: 'judge, jury, and executioner.' A lot of work – fourteen jobs in one. Who can blame these exhausted fellows and ma'ams for dressing in a nun's habit and a wig of adorable ringlets, and whacking their desk with a mallet whenever anyone tries to talk? It's a lot. We must appreciate the service of our judiciary, as we must honour the lesser lights of the justice system, from the lowly policeman or -woman 'beating the streets' to the swarthy gaoler with his ring of keys and steaming vats of gruel.

– Let's spend a moment on the police.

– Specifically, a moment of silence

– ...

– There.

– It's over.

– But the 'blue boys and girls' deserve greater honours than us simply shutting our mouths for one second literally. They're not just Bobbies anymore. Thanks to egalitarian hiring practices all varieties of nomenclature now grace the Badge, from Stevens and Akbars to Algernons, Tranhs, and Debbies – and beyond. My word, what a panoply! Meanwhile the police are cruising, or chopping past in their helicopters, or investigating crimes in trench coats, fedoras, and hangovers. Next time you see a copper or a little piggie trotting down the street, nightstick swinging, remember to tip your hat. Unless hats are illegal in your jurisdiction, in which case ... I don't know, tip your waitress instead.

– And what of prison? Underrated. One enjoys the merciful sanctity of a windowless cell, or a cell with a barred window to keep out the wolves and solicitors. The beds are cots, i.e. a web of coat hangers woven with delicate fluff. And the toilets are seatless for direct deposits. 'Paying for your crime' is achieved, in a curious irony, by living in prison rent-free. What a gift! As are group showers, in which no one is ever singled out for an exorbitant, unrequested dowry or a cavalcade of abuse emceed by a bearded genius. There's even soap. At mealtimes the prisoner need never feel paralyzed by choice, either, as they're just dolloped their portion of gruel and herded down the line.

– So there you have it. That's the justice system, from bottom (criminal) to top (ultimately, god), with the whole wondrous affair functioning in perfect harmony, like a finely luthiered lute. Strum those strings of justice, play us a harsh yet fair tune! Lovely. Now just pluck a single note, again and again, in a staccato rhythm meant to echo the careworn beating of our breaking, desperate hearts. *Twang. Twang. Twang. Twang.* Yes. There. Do you hear that? It's calling us with its siren song. Justice, that is. What's it saying? Just that it's coming for us – coming for us all, hungrily, like a murky tempest cresting the horizon, electric and ravenous and blackening with rage.

The day of the Trial began like any other, with a trip to Hut #7, which housed the communal toilets.

If I have not, to this point, mentioned much about the Retreat's 'facilities,' please consider this not a narrational failing, but rather a tactful, conscientious exclusion based in decency and decorum. Apologies if you are the noxious type who delights in personal ablutions and waste disposal. No judgment here, sicko. To each their own. Never mind, I suppose, that the public restroom shares many traits with Hell: both are asylums for people at their most derelict and despicable, where bodily atrocities implicate all involved, from perpetrator to involuntary witness, in enactments of sensory torture; also bowels.

So, leaving the specifics if not to the imagination (please resist envisaging yours truly kicking down the toilet seat, laying a mattress of toilet roll, etc.), then at least to the sewers of history – flushed away, that is, in a vortex of repudiation – I emerged from the bamboo-doored stall and moved outside to wash my hands. Collected around the taps in the morning sunlight were a half-dozen couples, who nodded at me decorously and continued to brush their teeth, apply rouges and lipsticks, pluck and/or shave errant and abhorrent hairs, decapitate 'heads' black and/or white, etc. The drains swirled pink with human and chemical effluents while I lathered and scrubbed.

Then something curious happened. Jerome came gliding down the path tethered to two hooded figures with a twenty-foot line. The villains Eye and Ewe! Emerged at last from custody, or captivity. Everyone stepped back from the trough to allow them access – not from respect or deference, but more the way a crowd will clear a path for a leper, lest they be oozed upon by one of its weeping, pustule sores.

The air stiffened.

– GREETINGS, said Jerome, wheeling up. THE ACCUSED ARE ENTITLED
TO WASH BEFORE TRIAL. REGARDS, JEROME.

– Please, I said, gesturing hospitably and stepping aside. By all means!

Jerome removed the hoods. I gasped. What emerged were less faces
than masks of tragedy. Blackened rings around the eyes suggested flogging
or exhaustion – or both. The lips, so chapped they had the corrugations
of bark, hung slackly open. The teeth within were chipped and brown.
The hair was at once grease-matted and frazzled, as if dipped in gravy
and lightly electrocuted. The cheeks, threaded with arterial fissures,
strained taut as clingfilm over the bones beneath. Such dereliction in a
scant two days!

Jerome ushered Eye and Ewe forward to the sinks. They staggered,
collapsed to their knees, opened the taps greedily and, with their wrists
still bound, began scooping water in feverish handfuls over their faces,
their heads, and into their mouths. This wasn't thirst. It seemed more
desperate, more absolute. I watched with a kind of morbid curiosity,
nudged at its edges with some darker compulsion – guilt, maybe, or shame.

And then they looked up and met my eyes across the trough.

What confronted me was not accusation. The eyes, amid the bruised
flesh that encircled them, were wide, haunted, questioning, imploring. In
them I saw a sequence that moved through disorientation, to recognition,
before landing on perplexity. No rage. Instead, like animals aware of their
imminent slaughter, they expressed only helpless, mystified pain. Anger
would have felt less impaling. This seeking, vacant, despairing look speared
me, hollowed me out, excavated my soul, found it empty, and called into
the abyss with a plaintive voice that echoed unanswered:

Why? Why? Why?

I couldn't take it. My hands still dripping, I backed away, forgoing the
Morning Activity (Brad Beard's 'Trust Game Olympics'), and fled to my
hut, where I collapsed on the waterbed like a jilted lover, which I suppose
I sort of was.

Sloshing about on my bed's rubbery surf, I eyed the dead screen of
the television. Dully floating upon that 'tube of boobs' was my own reflec-
tion, a lolling figure with the face of a ghost – stunned, disconsolate, lost.
I was meant to be the Advocate, a hero! The ceremonies I'd suffered had

confirmed me as such – a harbinger of justice, saviour of truth, and a towering figure of reverence and respect. Perhaps second only to the great Brad Beard, that king among pawns; I was at least his queen.

Wasn't I?

My televised mirror-self remained noncommittal. He returned my inquiry blankly, a question answered with another question. I began to squirm under his gaze, which echoed the despairing, beseeching expressions of the condemned Eye and Ewe.

I flopped back, mattress roiling tidally, and closed my eyes.

How I longed again for my wife – if not for consolation, then at least for company. And at the very, very least to feel a little less isolated with my torment. The hut seemed to thrum with a kind of latent energy, like the spent cocoon of some glorious butterfly that has evolved and escaped, fluttering off into the wild. Meanwhile here I remained, a lifeless, forsaken fish floating atop a churning, silky sea.

I sat up. The trial was to begin that afternoon, post-lunch – what Jerome was already referring to as the accused's LAST MEAL AND TESTA-MENT. (Apparently they'd requested, humbly enough, salads.) I had a few hours. Between me and my Dr. Dhaliwal, I knew, was a jungle both literal (the actual, terrifying, plant-based jungle) and metaphorical (emotions, bureaucracy, etc.). I had to conquer my fears – to break free from the cowardly prison that caged me, and to venture out as my wife had done, on my own, so that I might find her, and tell her everything was okay, and bring her home.

With the Morning Activity hosted in the Conference Room, the grounds of the Retreat appeared deserted. And despite the morning sun having lifted from nascent dither at the horizon to its current, searing omnipotence above the treeline, a chill seemed to chase me around back of the Welcome Centre, past, once again, the pool, the hot tub, and the hammocks, which trembled with the pathos of soiled bedding airing in the sea breeze.

At the trailhead I inhaled a breath of courage and plunged into the jungle, which closed around me like some monster's frondy gullet. But this was no time for figurative thinking; I had a very literal and explicit purpose: find my wife. Was Trunity still within our grasp? I could only pray that, reunited, we might reconcile, fuse our spirits, and join everyone else in Brad Beard's great communal mission to seek *the other side*.

Ignoring the hiss of vermin off in the bush and the jungly tendrils caressing me, I bore down the path with resignation. I cupped my hands over my cheeks so that my thumbs plugged my nostrils and my fingers shielded my ears (from fire-ants, from acid-fleas, from skull-worms), held my mouth tightly shut, hitched my robes into a snugly impenetrable lungi and clenched my buttocks. Nothing was getting in! Or out, besides the occasional grunt and/or whinge as I waddled grimly down the path.

At last the canopy thinned and the stone walls of the village towered ahead. I sprinted the last fifty metres and arrived gasping at the gates. Accepting my scanned wristband, the turnstile zapped, chirped, and permitted me through. Hesitantly I passed into the town square, wary that Jerome might have undertaken a solo shopping expedition here to purchase goods for the trial – signs quoting scriptural verses, noisemakers, fireworks, toy guillotines, etc. But the stalls were vacant. Not just of vendors and patrons, but goods as well. The silence and emptiness seemed, from my spot on its periphery, as composed and immutable as a landscape painting. To disturb it felt akin to tearing the canvas from its frame and attempting to chew myself inside.

Ever the refined aesthete, I paused.

Yet my wife was here, probably, somewhere. Art be damned. And enough inaction, enough fantasy, enough sloth! I had real goals to pursue in the real world. Fuelled by self-recrimination I charged into the square, past the assemblage of green heads lording sentry-like at its entrance. Chilling, certainly, but at least it remained platonically statuesque: the last thing I needed was the thing tumbling kinetically from its base and chasing me about town.

Roaming the market, I scanned the various corridors for passage into the village proper. I won't belabour my struggles as the sun ascended and baked the labyrinth and me blundering through it. Rest assured that by the time I located that escape hatch in the surrounding tarpaulin I was ravenous, sweaty, parched, sunburnt and approaching an intensity of impatience I'd previously harboured only for slowpokes at the toilets (what were they *doing* in there – hibernating?).

I found the village as abandoned as it had seemed upon our prior visit. The memory echoed with the subaquatic, hazy quality of an opiate-induced daydream. How much younger, more innocent, and (relatively) carefree I'd been then, with my wife at my side! Or, perhaps more accurately, with me trailing said wife through town in nervous mystery. Well, at least the nerves and mysteriousness had returned, albeit now in a more lonesome form.

I eyed my wife's coveted bell tower, lofting above town like a child's urgent hand amid a classroom of guilelessly idiotic peers. She was in there, I could sense it. Or I sensed something, which, while more probably the mild delirium of encroaching heatstroke, I chose to interpret as the telekinetic love-connection between husband (I) and wife (Dr. Dhaliwal). A mutual anthem, or shanty, that we crooned in harmony, though ideally not one that described me swept upon some rocky shoreline, my boat dashed to splinters, and my loins afire with mermaid-lust.

Wait, what boat? I was walking.

So I walked, the sun-fired cobblestones as scalding and bulbous as a mat of roast potatoes beneath my feet. Which is to say I less walked than danced, or skipped hectically on tiptoes, yelping with each scorching step. Why shoes, or at least socks, were not part of the Retreat's dress-code was beyond me. Wasn't the first rule of jungle survival *take care of your feet?* That and to avoid kissing snakes on the mouth, regardless how tantalizing.

After some twists and wrong turns, I emerged from a narrow laneway into that plaza with the chapel at the far end – the bell tower's shadow angling through the square like the needle of a massive sundial. But it was the guillotine, stationed upon the steps, its blade glinting in the sun, that commanded my immediate attention. Or, more so, the figure with its neck in the cradle. Someone dressed in the robes of the Retreat.

A chill slithered through me.

It was her. My wife. My love. My star! My summertime jamboree.

Dr. Dhaliwal: it had to be. Consigned to decapitation. How? Why?!

And then I noticed something else. The rope that held the blade aloft – balancing delicately, poised at any moment to drop and behead the woman below – fractured into a massive web that spread out over the square. Hundreds of filaments were each tied to some sort of eyelet or hitch anchored to the flagstones.

From my hiding place under a shop awning, I leaned into the light and peered closer.

And gasped.

Protruding from the ground were human fingers, curled like spent candlewicks, with the threads tied around the top knuckle. A few hundred of the things, planted in neat, ordered rows with the look of a paddy growing stout, fleshy shoots.

– I'm coming, I cried, stepping out of the shadows. Fear not, dear Dr. Dhaliwal!

She didn't so much as flinch. Too terrified probably. Or drugged? Dastards!

Instead what did move were the fingers. A dozen of the ones closest to me straightened to point in my direction – which in turn released the threads and sent the blade wobbling a few inches down.

I retreated hastily under the awning. My god! Not only had my foolhardy gesture risked beheading my wife, I'd been patently fingered in the process. Yet surely that was the lesser worry here, I told myself, as any good spouse would and should. More than the mortification of personal exposure, what required my focus here was not releasing the blade. I could not be the cause of my wife's headlessness. That was poor husbandry.

Surely fingers couldn't see, I reasoned, eyeing the great field of them embedded in the flagstones – half in shadow, half fairly glowing in the sunlight. They'd not seemed to detect my presence, despite how hotly I'd entered the plaza, until I'd shouted. So perhaps it was noise that triggered them. (How they might *hear*, of course, remains beyond me – but I don't make the rules, I just follow and report them.) If I could move silently around the plaza, I thought, perhaps I had a chance of freeing my wife.

I straightened slowly, ensuring that my robes didn't so much as rustle, and eyed the guillotine and its great lattice of fibres strung taut and fanning all around. There was only one thing to do, of course: mince.

It was time to mince as if my life depended on it. For it did.

And so, by god, I minced.

I minced like a man on a mission, which I was. A rescue mission! I was Dr. Dhaliwal's 'lord and saviour,' now, I felt – her 'one true hope.' So I tiptoed around the edge of the plaza, alternating glances between the robed outline of my wife in the shadow of the blade and all those precariously crooked fingers. Five steps out, then ten, turning the corner toward the chapel …

A half-dozen of the fingers, illuminated in a wedge of sunlight, seemed to quiver as I edged past. A kind of alerted waggling: *Lo! what have we here?* I paused, breath held, and waited for their fluttering to cease. The feeling was of walking by a pasture as the cows ogle you through the fence: what did they see? Anything? Or had cud-induced euphoria so astounded their senses that they were oblivious to anything beyond the sweet salve of regurgitated meadow?

The fingers stilled. And held. The blade remained in place.

I exhaled my breath in a great whoosh – and at this 'careless whisper' a dozen digits shot out in a stab of accusation. *You,* they seemed to scream, and point.

And the blade plummeted another six inches.

I nearly collapsed. Worthless! I couldn't even mince properly. I was no hero; I was a zero, a leery weirdo, a fraudulent faker, a hopeless nothing, a klutz, a doofus, a boor, a lout, a clumsy-dumbsy, a dink o' the month, Mr. Miscue, a wasted wastrel, a stumbling bumbler, a blundering blunderbuss, a bibulous butterfingers with two left feet and a headful of stupid-stones, a cat's sneeze, a ham-fisted porkpie, two honks short of a goose, a loafing oaf, a goofy picnic, a bad trip to the zoo, a rained-out parade, rude-and-crude, basic as a bulb, simple as a spoon, dull as a sandbag, beige-souled and crumple-butted and worthless, a dysfunctional disaster capable of at best scaling halfway to the heights of mediocrity and then gazing down from that unlofty perch at a world below indifferent to whether he soared or sank.

Or dropped.

Like a blade.

I blinked. (Quietly.)

Enough!

I shook these self-flagellating thoughts from my head – not literally, or physically, lest another reckless outburst imperil my wife further, but with a sort of brutal mental shove, stuffing all that insecurity into a back corner of my mind from which it could later be retrieved and properly engaged. And would, indisputably. But my wife needed me now.

So I moved, delicately – almost apologetically – to the next stone, and to the next, as silent and stealthy as a downy-footed panther. Without fail and without cease, and without another glimpse at the fingers or the strings or the deadly gleaming razor to which they were hitched. A kind of visual parsimony. Around the plaza, eyes on the prize: Dr. Dhaliwal. Who had put her there, I wondered? What sadistic barbarian had dared? My love, my partner, my soul, my bride – my Trunity. She'd complete me.

Each dainty, careful step brought me closer and closer still. The approach felt like negotiating a balance beam, except this fall wouldn't result in athletic defeat, but decapitation. My tiptoeing here was to achieve the ultimate podium: the one with my wife alive upon it.

I was so close now! A pace or two away!

Everything trembled in the light.

I stepped onto the pedestal alongside the guillotine, gasping in anticipation. After a brief pause to gather myself, I lunged forward to snatch my beloved from harm's way –

But I tripped. And barked my shin off the wooden base. And, at the blast of pain, forgetting myself, unleashed an obscene flurry of invective:

– *Dastard rotting blasting pooping guillotine, devil take you!*

At this every single one of the fingers snapped into turgid indictment, the whole web of tethers unfurled, and the blade came hurtling down. I jumped back as it thunked soundly below, slicing the figure below at the neck.

– No, I cried.

Too late. The head was severed. Because of me.

Stupid stupid!

And yet.

Instead of bouncing away like a fresh coconut lopped from the tree, the hood released gently and fluttered, like a leaf in the breeze, down to the flagstones below.

With no head inside.

I leapt forward and snatched the heap of robes from where they 'knelt.' Just cloth. No human within, never mind my wife. Empty. Discarded. And left there in a heap.

All that mincing … for nought.

At least Dr. Dhaliwal was alive. Probably? In dismay and desperation I gazed out over the plaza to the village beyond – ignoring the fingers below fondling the detached hood as if feeding on its fabric. Where the blazes was my wife? And what, I speculated with vicarious modesty, was she wearing?

I turned to face the chapel. The door was open – just a crack. The shadows within seemed to beckon or taunt me. I sniffed the air for Dr. Dhaliwal's scent, whatever it might have been. But I was no bloodhound. Simply a man. And I needed to become, once again, a man on a mission. So with yet another mental volta – that is, 'turning the other cheek' from my angst and disquiet to face the moment and the facts and my fears and, perhaps, the music (something elegant and choral, I hoped) – I puffed out my chest in a simulation of wherewithal, clasped my fists into punch-ready weapons, and pushed through the door of the chapel into the murky oblivion inside.

Through the crack in the door an isosceles of sunlight shone onto the chapel's stone floor. Beyond that loomed a starless galaxy. My attempt to widen that triangle – to heave open the door and carve a path through the dark – seemed to trip some sort of spring or safety mechanism. The thing slammed shut with a clap of thunder that reverberated up to the domed ceiling. I tried the handle: locked!

Turning, I squinted into air the colour of tar. Previously windows, I recalled, permitted slices of sunshine to glimmer down from the clerestory. But they were now shuttered or plugged, and the place was as lightless as the inside of a fist. I pictured its massive fingers unfurling like the limbs of a huge and hideous spider, and my wife's desiccated corpse, cocooned in corrosive silks, clasped in its drooling, hairy jaws.

No, I couldn't begin to speculate about monsters. For what was the world but a great menagerie of atrocities? What was the soul but a pit of snakes, i.e., despair? This chapel was simply another chamber in the 'horror house' of human existence. Around any corner might lurk demons or fiends or ogres or beasts, but wasn't that the case with every corner, everywhere? What hubris to fear what dwelled in this specific dark. The night was only unillumined day. The world remained the same, even with the lights off: the walls stayed in place, the ceiling arched above and nothing moved underfoot.

Or so I thought, striding blindly into the blackness – onto a floor that slid and oozed beneath my feet.

I yelped, jumped, sprung to a new spot. But it was the same here too. The tiles writhed. No, not tiles: the texture was fleshy and moist. I careened about in the darkness. Each step met that same damp and muscly parquet of flayed tissue, sticky and wriggling and warm. Finally I slammed into a wall and clawed along it, hoping I was tracing the interior of the chapel to the stairwell – somewhere to my right, if I remembered correctly. Meanwhile that seething mass underfoot creaked and slurped, and I feared that the stone walls to which I clung might, too, at any moment become slippery curtains of flesh.

Here it was: a gap, a doorway! I slipped through and bumped up against the bottom step of the tower: firm, concrete, not made of musculature, reassuringly vegetarian. Yet, recalling a banister fashioned from the same meaty material as the floor, I made sure to ascend with my hands before me in the fashion of sleepwalkers or the undead. Up I coiled, pawing the gloom, and up, and up, to whomever or whatever waited atop the tower. My wife? Ideally. Honestly, I'd have settled for a picturesque vista.

After a minute or two of climbing through the darkness, the space ahead of me began to pale. Sunlight! I accelerated, my heart hammering out an anxious tattoo. Rewards: more light spilled down from above with every step. I could see the walls, now, and the stairs beneath my feet. As I moved upward the stairwell further disclosed the noonday sun – the sun that had battered me since my arrival upon this island, but which now I hastened to embrace like a long-lost love. As, I imagined, with a flush of hope, I'd embrace my actual long-lost love, in a blaze of glory, atop the tower.

I rounded the final bend to a landing with a wooden door, yawing open. I pushed through with widened arms – for my wife to fall into, to hold her close.

But Dr. Dhaliwal didn't greet me. Though I wish she had. For what I discovered inside that room – well, I had imagined horrors. But none quite as chilling as this.

It was a room of skins.

Of full, human skins, at least from neck to toe. The heads had been removed, as had the fingers. Hundreds of the things, in all the ethnically coded colours of the human rainbow, and all the various shapes and sizes of the human form. Some of the hides looked as puckered as raisins, others appeared fresher – almost succulent. Some were hairy. Some were tall. Some were sallow, some tanned. Some were flappier and loose, recalling discarded sausage casings; some, despite lacking any interior support, bloated like overblown balloons. Piled as partygoers might heap coats on a bed (or so I imagine; my invitations thus far in life seemed to have been 'lost to the mail') and illuminated by sunshine through the window.

A cloud interrupted the sunlight. And as the room darkened, so did my thoughts: this is what my wife had seen, what had motivated her disappearance. This museum of epidermal horror, of the beheaded and unfingered and eviscerated. Just like Tubbing's better, deader half. And so she'd – what? How did revelation become action, when my impulse was to close the door, back away, and never again think of what I'd seen?

A noise from below interrupted my ruminations, such as they were. A kind of moaning.

I recalled that Dr. Dhaliwal had, on our previous visit, located a light switch. I scanned the walls, spotted a dimmer by the door, leapt forward, and cranked it clockwise. The stairwell glowed as if lit with a signal-fire.

Another moan wafted up from the chapel, plaintive and sustained, like the lowing of a mournful yet sonorous porpoise. Or, I hoped, a recently feral wife's mating call – that is, the call she unleashed to the wilds to summon her estranged, ever-loving mate.

Eight

Moaning, was it? Or, as I discovered upon attaining the ground floor and came thumping out into the chapel, more a kind of groaning?

I deploy these questions facetiously, for the purposes of rhetoric.

Indeed it was groaning.

A collective groaning! The pews were full, and lit garishly by a stained-glass chandelier, with Retreaters who groaned and rocked like a caucus of the ulcered and petulant. The domed ceiling seemed to swell with the chromatic ascensions of that requiem of collective spleen, while I stood in the stairwell's doorway, eyeing the exit – a lunge-and-scuttle away from freedom.

But then a voice implored them for silence:

– QUIET IN THE COURT, PLEASE. REGARDS, MY HONOUR, JEROME.

And so they were silent.

In the shadows behind the altar I spied him now, the shepherd to his groaning flock: that stalwart column, head sparkling with greenish lights. He saw me too.

– THE ADVOCATE ARRIVES, he declared. REGARDS, MY HONOUR, JEROME.

The congregation swivelled in their seats, catching me edging toward escape.

– Hurrah! exclaimed the lot of them. *Hurrah, hurrah! / Murderers, blah! / The Advocate's here to end the foofaraw!*

– Indeed, I said, nodding sagely, stepping into the light, literally, of the chandelier, but also figuratively: that is, the light of their adoration, their hope, their dreams, their life, their days, their world, their Retreat. And now their trial.

– Yes, I continued, thank you. I am the Advocate. And I am here. And so are you.

They seemed to want more.

So I gave it to them, with Beardian bombast:

– The Trial commences anon!

And bowed, and curtsied.

I'd anticipated applause. There wasn't any. I straightened to two dozen heads pivoting back to the altar in bemusement. And this jostled loose a memory: the figures my wife and I had seen sitting in those same pews. Hunched, I'd believed at the time. But now, with an explicit visual counterpoint, I realized they'd been headless.

So: a beheaded mob, a courtyard of fingers, a roomful of skins; a statue of skulls, a fingerless body, a widower in a skin-cape. The variables jostled against each other, but there was no time to wrangle them into order – Jerome was summoning me to the altar.

At a table to his left sat the hooded defendants, Eye and Ewe; to his right was my empty throne. Sighing, I lowered myself into its cushy confines and waited to be buckled in. For once, I was spared. Yet any confidence attendant to my rank of Advocate extinguished in a great gust of panic, like a match snuffed by a lugubrious wind.

My argument! The one I'd so painstakingly crafted in the video 'Liberarry.' I'd left it upon the nightstand in my hut. The battle was pending and here I sat, at the frontlines, without armour or weaponry. I fumbled through the folds of my robes, as if I might conjure those pages via fondling. My hands emerged empty. And as I sat there, with the crowd percolating with expectation, dismay blazed up through my guts, sizzled down my limbs and exploded hotly in my fingers and toes.

Perhaps you have suffered some correlative nightmare, in which certain triumph is usurped by foolishness, ill-preparation, or slack-brained oversight. A nursing exam for which you'd only studied techniques for smoking ham; a rousing public address unintentionally delivered in buttock-flapped chaps; or a turn as star prosecutor to which, due to a well-intentioned but foolhardy attempt to locate your estranged wife, you'd failed to bring your notes, so the throne upon which you perched felt less regal than a stage for humiliation, like some tomato-splattered pillory or 'selection row' at the orphanage.

As the crowd's restless groaning resumed, and Jerome again called for order, I struggled to recall what I'd written, to summon the first sentence and then carom from it to the next, and so on, all the way to my immaculate, incontrovertible conclusion. Yet the words dissolved. My arguments became the dews of morning sunbaked to vapour, and I was left grasping at their wispy tendrils.

I glanced across the aisle, but Eye and Ewe's head-sacks revealed nothing. The spectators hushed, finally, as Jerome ushered the trial into its opening gambits.

–TO BEGIN, JEROME, MY HONOUR, WILL INTRODUCE THE COUNSEL FOR THE DEFENCE, intoned Jerome. WE KNOW HIM AS THE AUTHOR OF YOU ARE NOT NO THING AND THE SUBJECT OF MULTIPLE FAILED LAWSUITS, SO PLEASE GIVE A WARM WELCOME TO … SOLICITOR BRAD BEARD! REGARDS, MY HONOUR, JEROME.

From the wings, waving garrulously, trotted the man himself. He slid in front of Jerome, blowing kisses to the standing ovation that thundered through the chapel – or courtroom, now, per its tribunal retrofit. Even Eye and Ewe did their best to clap along, which their handcuffs limited to spastic shrugging; their bagged heads nodded like batted-about balloons.

– Thank you, Jerome, your Honour, began Brad Beard, his tone greying as he gestured for his worshippers to lower into the pews. But rather than advancing his opening statement he began pacing a pensive circle, his hands clasped behind his back. The classic pose of the philosopher! Then Beard wheeled like a gunslinger, his forefinger aimed at my heart.

– I would like to direct my first remarks to or about the Advocate, who we all know and love, no doubt about it. But who really is the Advocate?

I grinned blamelessly, my head wobbling as if to evade a hail of microscopic bullets.

– Who, continued Solicitor Beard, *is* the Advocate? *Who* is *he*? Or whom?

– Mr. Dhaliwal? I squeaked.

– OBJECTION! OVERRULED! intervened Jerome. REGARDS, MY HONOUR, JEROME.

– Overrulement sustained, your Honour, gloated Beard, chuckling sadly. Sustained indeed. It's been a sustained mystery, for me at least, for the past several days. Has anyone else wondered about this guy? Sure, he's a real pillar of salt, anyone can see that. I mean, if you cut him he'll bleed out red like any of us. Platelets and whatnot, plasma …

– Let's rend his flesh! screamed someone from the back of the room. Brad Beard held up his hands. – Well whoa there now, Slicey McDicey. Laughter. Nervous and relieved.

– Keep your knives in the drawer. I'm not saying we should … *cut* … the Advocate. But I think in the interest of a free and fair trial here we should at least start with what we do and don't know. And, you know? I don't know about this Advocate, one bit. Do you?

I realized that as he spoke he'd been slinking, lithe and catlike, toward me. Now he stood right before my throne. He leaned down, his hands gripping the armrests. He was so close I could smell the butter in his beard. My god, so much butter.

– Who are you, he whispered, *really*?

– Just a guy, I tried. Just an Advocate kind of guy!

But Brad Beard simply stared. I realized he was lifting the throne, tipping it backward on two legs so I tilted back. Would he 'dump' me? Did he dare? What sort of legal strategy was that? But after letting me dangle perilously for a moment, he simply released his grip and returned the throne to the floor with a boom like cannon fire. I nodded a simple thanks.

– No further questions, your Honour, said Beard, and backed away with his hands raised in a gesture of disavowal, or renunciation. Of almost, I feared, certain victory.

– THANK YOU, SOLICITOR BEARD, said Jerome, once the ovation had subsided. YOUR TURN, THE ADVOCATE. REGARDS, MY HONOUR, JEROME. Rather than join his clients, Brad Beard elected to move beside Jerome, one hand paternally cupping the robot's domed head. Standing, I straightened my robes. A hush had, as they say, descended. Though, no: this hush had not drifted down from above in the fashion of alpine mist, but seemed to leach up from the concrete floor, gaseous and sinister, like the effluent from a septic tank. A sulfuric smell even accompanied it, one I chose to attribute to the Retreat's notoriously eggy breakfasts.

I faced the defendants. Beneath the hoods I could picture the same searching gaze they'd fixed upon me at the taps that morning. I looked away – but there was nobody and nothing to look at that didn't indict me. The whole room felt seized with anticipation, albeit the morbid sort one experiences unleashing a wounded bird from a balcony: will it fly? Or simply detonate below in a gruesome explosion of feathers and viscera?

Something was expected of me. Yet no longer something grand, worthy of the title of Advocate. This was more apprehensive – perversely so. I felt like the unlucky plane crash survivor elected to provide a banquet of his own flesh, yet my tools for butchery were only plastic spoons. Though what choice did I have? Better to just dig in, I thought, as I lifted my chin and, in the manner of a new castrato's first solo, allowed my mouth to open, to unleash whatever impromptu ignominies might dwell within.

I shall not belabour with quotation the ludicrous soliloquy that followed, nor even paraphrase its aphasic stutterings and the legless flop of its syntactical gymnastics. Instead I shall itinerate the series of animations that played upon Jerome's head as I spoke, by which I hope to convey not only the linguistic and logistical goulash I slopped about the room but how it was duly, stupefyingly received.

These proceeded as follows:

Smile.

Fading smile.

Mouthless face.

Question mark.

Question mark.

Question mark.

Interrobang.

Two interrobangs.

Wince.

A fisherman casting into a puddle and hooking himself in the eye.

Said eye dangling from a fish hook, plucked free by an intrepid seagull.

The same seagull at the dump showing the eyeball to his friends (unimpressed).

The eyeball floating out to sea while a fisherman staggers about the shoreline in an eyepatch.

Question mark.

Laughter.

Tears of laughter.

Sobbing.

Wiping away tears.

Recalibration.

Unblinking stare.

Unblinking stare.

Shaking head of perplexity.

Shaking head of awe.

Shaking head of worry.

Shaking head of vicarious mortification.

Slumped head.

A coffin.

Heaven. Angels. Harps.

Question mark.

Interrobang.

Shrug.

A hand slapping a forehead.

The scales of justice.

Question mark.
Exclamation mark.
Ellipsis. (looped)
Someone checking their watch.
Ellipsis. (looped)
An ad for Brad Beard's AbBuster 3000™.
A stop sign.
Interrobang.
Hands clasped in prayer.
Someone sleeping, plus scrolling Z's.
The scales of justice.
Shrug.
'FIN.'

Perhaps it wasn't all so bad, I thought, returning to my throne. I did feel exhausted. Surely that suggested at least mental and emotional effort – and weren't points awarded for trying? I peeked over my shoulder to gauge how my address had landed. Had I 'pleased the court'? Every head hung low. In reverence? Was the silence that clasped the room one in which every last attendee – Jerome, Beard, and the accused included – were simply basking in the splendour of my oration?

Unlikely.

What had I even said? What were 'the caramels of righteousness?' What had I meant by 'ten shiny sap-shanks into life's barky truth-tree?' Whom was I addressing when I'd shifted to the second person and screamed, 'a pox on your dad's doodads!' Retrospectively treading through each lunatic phrase felt like hopping barefoot across a bed of thistles – which I'd planted myself. Across that turf of gnarly pricks my thoughts leapt and cringed until returning, at last, to the throne where I now slumped with all the despair of a ruined, unworthy king.

From the silence emerged shuffling, fidgeting, toe-tapping, phlegmatic snortling, a snarf of ahems, a chorus of tired, sad sighs. I sensed a further realignment of allegiances. Despite the authority of my title, Brad Beard's piercing invective offered passage upon a dependable barge over the river of justice – versus my leaky dinghy foundering rudderless into the torrents.

Upon Jerome's head flashed a scorecard:

BEARD: 29; ADVOCATE: −4

– ROUND ONE, Jerome tallied, SOLICITOR BEARD. REGARDS, MY HONOUR, JEROME.

The cheers this inspired felt aggressively partisan. Only one, trembling voice offered anything like encouragement, or solidarity, after the triumphant howls had faded.

– Come on, the Advocate! You can do it!

Tubbing – waving so vigorously his leathery poncho rippled like a stingray. I nodded thanks and took stock: I would dedicate any subsequent testimony to the man who had once been my ally, even if his support was obviously sarcastic.

– AND NOW, said Jerome, WE BEGIN ROUND TWO: RE-ENACTMENTS. REGARDS, MY HONOUR, JEROME.

Brad Beard stepped forward, hands tented at his chin in a kind of thespian prayer. A theatrical component? Unfair! Even if I'd brought my notes I'd have been outmatched; Beard had got his start as one half of the sketch comedy duo Crush 'n' Bruise. (Apparently he still broke out 'Boneless Harry' at private functions.)

And, my god, here it came! Beard extended his arms into a crucified T, closed his eyes, slowly drew his hands to his sides, inhaled so deeply he seemed to imbibe the spirit of dramaturgy itself, dropped to the floor with a fist clenched at his forehead, and finally flew into a pantomime of such acuity, elegance, and urgency that I'd only cheapen it by trying to transmute its corporeal power into language.

Did Brad Beard 'act'? No, Brad Beard *was*.

Specifically: Brad Beard danced.

Brad Beard danced, and he danced the truth. Not simply *his* truth, but every dainty flounce and recumbent scuttle seemed to express some elemental truth about all of us – Advocate and accused, human and robot, Tubbing and skin-cape, Sayer and Beard himself. It was riveting; it was real. The only sounds were the shushing of bare feet over the stone floors and the dancer's slight gasps as he contorted and writhed from one sequence to the next. Everyone watched in total, riveted silence. Agog. Rapt.

This was Trunity: embodied, exemplified, and alive.

What Solicitor Beard's dance represented wasn't so much an argument for his clients' innocence – he didn't sink to the literal banalities of events, plots, actions, details, and so on – but more an interpretive expression of the very notion of facts. For what was reality, I wondered, as Brad Beard flagellated around the room in the manner of something single-celled and subaquatic. How could one ever really say what happened, to whom, how or when or where or why? Our edifier and master, shimmying into the pews like a loose and gooey noodle, seemed to suggest that we were all just so much ephemera, battered about like, yes, a noodle on – what? the winds of time? the seas of hope, or fear, or change? the clam-sauce of lost and broken dreams?

From here Beard transitioned to his grand finale, arms pinwheeling and legs pistoning as he came careening back to the altar. My god, he looked positively Soviet! So strident and severe, with an icy glaze to the eyes that spoke of the terrors of the steppe. What had he seen? What *did* he see, now, gazing upon us? Nothing, I thought, as Brad Beard's feverish, possessed presentation began to slow into an almost pensive denouement, one that illuminated the grandest and most painfully profound truth yet: we were all of us nothing, I knew now – nothing at all.

The arms stilled. The legs calmed. Soon he was simply tapping a toe, cradling himself with both arms.

Tap, tap, tap.

Tap. Tap.

Tap.

And then he simply stood there, breath heaving.

It was over.

No applause followed. Even as Brad Beard returned alongside Jerome, everyone simply gawked in awe and divine revelation. We had all witnessed something, we knew, whose effects were to leave us all irrevocably, irresolutely changed. Perhaps in ways we would not discover for days, or months, or years; perhaps in ways we would never consciously apprehend. But for now what lingered was a sense of life-altering epiphany. To clap or cheer risked shattering its cosmic spell.

Yet 'the show,' as they say, 'must goon.' And it was my turn to play said goon.

– THANK YOU, SOLICITOR BEARD, said Jerome. AND NOW, THE ADVOCATE, YOU MAY OFFER YOUR REBUTTAL. REGARDS, MY HONOUR, JEROME.

I stood, I nodded, I shrugged, I paused.

But how could I follow that? Jazz hands?

Fine: a listless, four-second outburst of jazz hands.

Gratuitously, I felt, Jerome proclaimed a victory for the defence and displayed the score for the second round.

BEARD: ∞; ADVOCATE: NOUGHT.

I'd dug quite a hole, down two rounds to none. Yet I was nothing if not a fighter!

Well, to be truthful, I was many things if not a fighter … I just hoped I could be those things *as well as* a fighter. Could an irresolute coward be a fighter? Yes, one could fight by cowardly means. But could one win a fight with cowardice? Perhaps not with it – but in its spite? Or could one, I thought, straightening upon my throne, *exploit* one's cowardice to discomfit the opposition, especially if said opposition were courageous and valiant and as virulently bearded as a Hun, and as such accustomed to battles with a commensurately brave adversary in which one struck and parried blows, and leapt about shouting heroic phrases like 'on guard!' and 'your tit for my tat!' and 'Avast, ye merry gentleman!' and, pausing climactically before the final death-strike, 'This … ends … *now.*'

I'd been approaching the whole trial misguidedly. Traditional competition with Brad Beard was a mistake. Might he instead be bewildered, and bested, with irreverence? If I were to claim victory it would only be sneakily, through wily, improbable, and unpredictably bizarre strategies and techniques. I needed to embrace my idiosyncrasies and foibles, not flee them.

And so, as Jerome signalled the beginning of round three –

– THE CROSS-EXAMINATION. REGARDS, MY HONOUR, JEROME.

– and I was called 'to the stand' (as in, to stand up and start talking), I rose gingerly, per my usual countenance. But then I shocked them all by clucking.

– Bock, I cried. Bock, bockaw! Cock-a-doodle-doo! Kikiriki! Cocorico!

And so forth, flapping my elbows seductively and wing-like. A mating call! A call of lusty conquest and/or availability! I thrust my forehead to the ceiling, cawing mightily, and displayed my titillating pate as an ample roost or perch.

And a cry replied:

– Bockaw!

The crowd's collective gaze shot upward: out of the rafters swooped the Boss, my old and somewhat constant companion. Down she soared with prototypical elegance, like a fluffy kite descending a subtle draft, and alit, as was her wont, upon the crown of my head. And there she perched, as proud and vain as a chicken, or hen, could be.

– Now *lay*, damn you, I hissed. Lay!

I felt feathers ruffle, a muscular seizure, a kind of bracing. Wiggling. Loosening. Oh, and there it was, out it squirmed … Warm and oblong and perfect. I reached up, wormed my fingers under the Boss's tailfeathers and fetched what she'd deposited there. And held it aloft for all to see. Wonder and appreciation purred through the court.

And then I thrust that fresh, hot egg at the accused.

– What, Mr. Eye and Mrs. Ewe, is this?

– We can't see, protested a meek voice from one of the hoods.

– Ah. Precisely!

I turned to the audience, 'Exhibit A' displayed between my thumb and index finger.

– An egg, I descanted, is many things. White, like this specimen here. But sometimes brown. Speckled, occasionally, or flecked. I've seen eggs blue and green, as you might have had to suffer as well. But I think we can agree of one constant between every egg – penguin and salamander, python and platypus. And human too, i.e., the ovum. Not caviar, though; that's something else.

I allowed them a moment to contemplate what might come next. But I pre-empted their prognostications with a surge of rhetorical flourish:

– An egg, I screamed, every egg, is only ever potential. What lurks within this shell? A life? An omelette? A clotted stillborn fetal muck? It could be anything. Until we smash through its protective sheath what awaits inside is limited only by our imaginations. Why, if I claimed that within this very egg spouted a font of liquid gold, who would you be to argue? Especially if I claimed that oxygen would turn said elixir into useless albumen.

Nods of agreement, of acquiescence to my unassailable logic. And, just when my audience felt themselves settling into some sort of conventional locutionary flow, I disrupted them again:

– Well let's find out!

I dashed the egg upon the stone floor. A yellow explosion! Everyone gasped!

– You see? We'll never know what might have been. And all we have to show for it is this oozing mess. Can we return our egg to pure potential? Can we put it back together again? We cannot. Try as you might. Assemble all the regalest horses and men in the kingdom, and while they're scrambling about, that thing will rot like a corpse. The smell alone will drive you to fits. And isn't that what life is? Here today, decaying tomorrow? As with our dear friend Tubbing's spouse, once so mighty, now little more than a limp sheet pinned to his widower's shoulders … The work, mind, of these two hooded maniacs seated so blithely, and dare I say arrogantly, before the court. Who wears a hood to trial? Only a guilt-ridden predator with something to hide. Well, gaze upon your handiwork, creeps: here wilts its scraps upon the shoulders of good Tubbing! Those flappy remains of our poor, dead comrade, cored like an apple. Emptied … like a broken egg.

I glared, in silence, at the gelatinous puddle on the floor. Its star-shaped, golden-hued splatter might have been a child's rudimentary artistic rendering of our own sun. (The bits of shell were meteorites and space-dust, clearly.) But, more so, I wanted everyone to recognize what we were truly looking at: an allegory of time – its relentless forward march; its irrevocability; its explosive, fantastic end.

– Make no mistake, I cautioned in a voice of cold steel, that we cannot allow the fashioning of a 'human omelette' to go unpunished. For if we do, we are failing not just Tubbing and his disembowelled husband, or the poultry industry, or even justice itself …

With pity and foreboding I gazed beyond the crowd, as if glimpsing what awaited them at the horizon of their doomed, forsaken lives. When my silence had amplified into adequately bathetic registers, I reached up once more under the hen on my head, plucked free a second egg and displayed it for all to see.

– If we fail here, today, my friends?

I paused again; my pacing was masterful. Such suspense! Behind me, I could sense a consternated Brad Beard 'eating out his own heart.' I grinned and concluded, with a rousing finish to rival any grand epic or symphony:

– Your own beloved eggs … *will be next.*

And I hurled 'Exhibit B' at the floor.

Though this time the shell did not splinter and split. Instead it popped like a balloon, and that porcelain exterior withered into limp foil. And what emerged was not another yolk, but a moth or butterfly, fluttering into a shaft of light and dithering there, wings flapping steadily.

Yet a butterfly it was not.

In place of wings wagged a pair of human ears, stitched together at the openings to their respective canals. Two ears, in symmetry, beating the air to stay aloft. And, gathering itself, this curious hatchling seemed to catch an updraft, performed a brief loop-de-loop, and then went thrashing up into the rafters of the chapel, where it vanished into that lightless pit carved high above.

– What the freak-darned hell was *that*? shouted Brad Beard. I can't, there's
no words. It's like being handed a hamper of laundry and told 'rate this
supper.' No, I won't be rebutting whatever that phony-baloney was. Eggs?
Ears?! No further questions, Your Honour.

  – ROUND THREE TO THE ADVOCATE, THEN, BY DEFAULT, announced
Jerome. His head flashed DEFAULT: ADVOCATE WINS. THE TRIAL IS NOW
TWO ROUNDS TO SOLICITOR BEARD, AND ONE TO THE ADVOCATE. AND
NOW WE BEGIN THE FOURTH ROUND: THE DRAWING OF STRAWS. REGARDS,
MY HONOUR, JEROME.

  Out shot Jerome's tray. Upon it were two straws. Brad Beard, already
close by, snatched the longer of the two. Thrusting it skyward in triumph,
he hooted.

  – Beard for the win!

Pitifully, wretchedly, I slunk over, and fetched the lesser straw, and
retreated. With a mocking laugh Beard brandished his selection, a shaft
of plastic as long as a dagger, showily jousted the air and twirled it between
his fingertips like a baton. Now the whole crowd was chanting.

  – *Beard, Beard, Beard! / Turns out the Advocate's weird! / His straw's so small /
It's almost not-at-all / Unlike Brad Beard's which is really long and great.*

  Jerome's tray retracted.

  I stood there with that plastic nub concealed in my fist, while the
Retreaters' pro-Beard mantra washed over me. Meanwhile Eye and Ewe
sat numbly in place behind their table. Motionless. Almost corpselike, as
if propped up in their chairs. I peered more intently, surprising myself at
this sudden investment in their well-being. After all, the express purpose
of my Advocacy was to dispatch them to their slaughter. I felt relief when
I detected the sacks quivering around the accuseds' nostrils. Still alive.
For now. And, with Beard having pulled the long straw, perhaps forever.

Well, not forever, obviously. For all of us are loaded at birth onto a conveyor belt that slurps us to our invariable end: cerebral hemorrhage, probably, and a naked collapse on our kitchen floor, where in the following weeks bloat and mouldering reek and flesh-devouring parasites will consume our bodies, before we might be discovered by a neighbour on an innocent hunt for a cup of sugar, who vomits all over our decomposing corpse before fleeing to the street, screaming in revulsion. Then: collection, cremation, and our gritty remains decanted into a plastic bag forgotten between the grass seed and rat poison in some distant relative's garage. Life!

Curiously, Jerome had not announced a victory for the Defence. Instead, his tray popped open again. Upon it was a box about the size of a wordy thesaurus. Pink, with a gold clasp. And a locket.

– PLEASE, said Jerome, SOLICITOR BEARD, SINCE YOU DREW FIRST, YOU MAY ATTEMPT TO OPEN THE BOX OF DELIGHTS WITH YOUR STRAW-KEY. REGARDS, JEROME.

Brad Beard eyed in turn the box, his straw, and me, and my straw. And laughed. And swaggered forward with all the moxie of a small-town mayoral incumbent cutting the ribbon on a new bridge or necropolis.

– No sweat, Jerome. I've got just the thing right here.

Yet when he tried to slot his straw into the lock, the thing simply crinkled in his hand: too big, too long, too abundantly tipped! Brad Beard, incredulous and unaccustomed to failure and/or rejection, tried again to insert his too-long key with greater force – eliciting similar results. Each subsequent, increasingly violent attempt only heightened his frustration and deepened his frown. By the end, a kind of collective, vicarious embarrassment had settled over the court as we watched him, in the widened stance of a calving heifer, mashing his straw into plastic splinters that littered the floor.

Only then did he turn, eyeing me distastefully, as if I were the mastermind of his misfortune. With an ironic, gratuitous sweep of his arm he invited me forward.

– Please, Mr. Advocate, why don't you and your baby-stick take a crack at it.

Nodding modestly, I stepped up. The box sat on Jerome's tray gouged with scars from Brad Beard's botched probing. What did I have to lose? (The trial, my dignity – my life?) I eased my nub up to the keyhole, held my breath, and attempted an insertion.

My god, with a click the lid popped open!

Out came the tinkling melody of a music box. And in the centre, upon a rotating dais, spun a figurine: a miniature version of the cerebral statue that had vanished from the town square. A little stack of tiny green heads, spinning daintily to a dirgelike tune.

Jerome spoke:

– ROUND FOUR TO THE ADVOCATE. REGARDS, MY HONOUR, JEROME.

The crowd offered a polite, appreciative, if hardly vehement, round of applause as Jerome displayed the score:

ADVOCATE: 1; BEARD: 0

– THAT'S TWO ROUNDS TO THE ADVOCATE, AND TWO ROUNDS TO SOLICITOR BEARD. A DRAW. AND SO, TO DECIDE THE FATE OF THE ACCUSED, WE MUST HAVE A FINAL, DECISIVE ROUND: SUDDEN DEATH. THIS WILL TAKE PLACE IN THE PLAZA OUTSIDE. REGARDS, MY HONOUR, JEROME.

And on the figurine twirled, and on that strange song jingled, as the Retreaters rose and filed out of the chapel. Other than Jerome, I was the last to join them, emerging alongside the guillotine under an inferno of mid-afternoon sunshine that, without shade or shelter from its ceaseless, raging incandescence, nakedly scorched and torched us all.

Remarkably, it was Professor Sayer who inaugurated the event's final round, stepping to the front of the guillotine's platform, appraising the attended masses with a hand on her heart, or bosom, and then offering the following address:

– As you all know, I am, yes, Professor R.G. Sayer, MPhil, PhD, your in-house and resident counsellor, as well as, now, the official Executrix for this portion of the day's entertainment, or judicial proceedings, whatever, of the Advocate versus, as represented by our own garrulous, silver-tongued and supremely gifted Bradley J. Beard, Mr. Eye and Mrs. Ewe, who are, I should qualify, only the *alleged* accused, no guilt has been proven, yet, in the gruesome murder, and tragic loss, and gory evacuation, of the body, soul, and mind of one of our very own, here at the Retreat, a trial which, already, has offered a truly exhilarating, scene-stealing performance of criminal defence, not to mention heroism, by Solicitor Beard, and who could have predicted our allegiances to swing, so dramatically, from initial, naively instinctive support for the prosecution, per the Advocate's assumed authority and credibility, buoyed by the position's storied and gallant history, now tested, if not compromised, by whatever that business was with the eggs, I'm still confused, not to mention the arguments so exquisitely presented by the shatteringly charismatic Solicitor Beard, who has, I think we can all agree, aroused, among other things, our sympathies for the accused, whose hooded visages strike us now as the faceless lot of victims, which, in turn, forces us to wonder, I think, who the real monster might be, perhaps those who seek to mete blame, and point fingers, and yet, due to the Advocate's implausible, come-from-behind, late-round revival against Solicitor Beard, that wunderkind of oral technique, here we are, Sudden Death, that most terminal of rounds, in which truth will lubricate the orifices of jurisprudence, and into those slickened cavities will penetrate the stiff, turgid authority of a verdict, so let's begin, thank you.

   – THANK YOU, PROFESSOR SAYER, said Jerome, rolling forward. SUDDEN DEATH IS NOT A HEAD-TO-HEAD MATCHUP, BUT SIMPLY A TEST OF THE ADVOCATE'S ABILITIES AND FORESIGHT. AND SO, THE ADVOCATE, WE ADMINISTER THE COWL OF DESTINY. REGARDS, MY HONOUR, JEROME.

   I was seized from behind. The pungent odour of buttered beard momentarily filled my nostrils, extinguished as a burlap sack was thrust over my head and knotted at my chin. I couldn't see! Or, rather, all I could see – and smell – was sack.

   – NOW LET'S GET THE ADVOCATE IN PLACE. REGARDS, MY HONOUR, JEROME.

   Those manly hands took me by the shoulders, manoeuvred me across the platform, forced me down to my knees, and then tilted me at the waist, forward, into the kneeling posture of a supplicant.

   – THAT'S IT, THE ADVOCATE: PLACE YOUR NECK IN THAT CRADLE. EXCELLENT. ALL SET AND READY FOR SUDDEN DEATH. REGARDS, MY HONOUR, JEROME.

   – My god, I cried, sightless and kneeling, my head lolling over a wooden ledge. Am I under the guillotine?

   – You're dang right, intoned the voice of Brad Beard. Best of luck, the Advocate!

   – WHILE JEROME APPRECIATES YOUR ENTHUSIASM FOR SUDDEN DEATH, SOLICITOR BEARD, PLEASE ALLOW JEROME TO ELUCIDATE THE PROCEDURES WITHOUT INTERRUPTION. REGARDS, MY HONOUR, JEROME.

   I waited. Shuffling sounds moved around the platform – and stilled. And then, for a moment, all was as vindictively silent as the blazing sun above, which roasted my supine, upturned rear-end almost sarcastically. Finally Jerome spoke again:

   – THE ADVOCATE, THE COWL OF DESTINY IS ADORNED WITH A BOBBLE OF GUILT. YOU MUST WITHDRAW AT THE PRECISE MOMENT SO THE FALLING BLADE SEVERS THE BOBBLE. IF YOU DO SO CORRECTLY, YOU WILL WIN SUDDEN DEATH, KEEP YOUR HEAD, AND THE ACCUSED WILL BE PUNISHED IN YOUR STEAD. PULL OUT TOO SOON AND JEROME WILL PUSH YOU BACK. AND, OBVIOUSLY, PULL OUT TOO LATE: SUDDEN DEATH. ANY QUESTIONS? YOU ARE PERMITTED ONE. REGARDS, MY HONOUR, JEROME.

   – I'm sorry, I cried, *what*?

— THE ADVOCATE, THE COWL OF DESTINY IS ADORNED WITH A BOBBLE OF GUILT. YOU MUST WITHDRAW AT THE PRECISE MOMENT SO THE FALLING BLADE SEVERS THE BOBBLE. IF YOU DO SO CORRECTLY, YOU WILL WIN SUDDEN DEATH, KEEP YOUR HEAD, AND THE ACCUSED WILL BE PUNISHED IN YOUR STEAD. PULL OUT TOO SOON AND JEROME WILL PUSH YOU BACK. AND, OBVIOUSLY, PULL OUT TOO LATE: SUDDEN DEATH. YOU ARE NOW OUT OF QUESTIONS. REGARDS, MY HONOUR, JEROME.

— But —

— YOU ARE NOW OUT OF QUESTIONS. REGARDS, MY HONOUR, JEROME.

So this is how it would end: head-bagged and genuflecting before a crowd of bloodthirsty onlookers, my head lopped off like a lawnmowered dandelion. In the darkened hutch of that itchy hood, I tried to summon some last words – something rousing and noble by which to be remembered. As Brad Beard had once demanded: Who was I, really? An excellent question, I thought. Yet no words came. And, anyway, my elegy was preempted by Professor Sayer.

— If I may, Jerome, Your Honour, please, before we begin, as Executrix I'd like to elicit a round of applause for Solicitor Beard, thank you, everyone, let's hear it, let's honour the man's stalwart, commanding presence, which has guided us all, collectively, toward Trunity, and beyond, and we're so close, can't you all feel it, I think it's here, this is the moment, we're all together, the Advocate awaits his fate, and so do we, and I'll just remind the fellow with his head on the line that Jerome is right behind you with his shoving mechanism poised, should you try to jump free pre-emptively, and now, without further ado, please let me assume the position, oh, Brad, you naughty devil, I saw that lurid little look, there's plenty of time for that later, after the Advocate's Sudden Death, and, Jerome, it's this lever here, is it, to release the blade, yes, excellent, there we are, everything's ready, here we go, and just to update you, the Advocate, Jerome's begun the countdown on his display screen, though from what number of course I can't tell you, and I'm ready to flip the switch, as they say, at zero, and best of luck, we're all cheering for you, but enough talk, let's follow those numbers, down and down we go, the Advocate, pick your moment, you can do it, a lot's at stake for you, yes, let's see what happens, everyone, now, *the other side* awaits us all.

Nine

Kneeling there with my head in the block, with nothing visible but that murky crosshatch of burlap, I became acutely and abruptly aware of my neck. That column of spine-braced meat: how little regard I'd paid it for so long, and how significant it suddenly seemed. So peripheral to our attention, necks – not like the hotshot satellites on either end, the head and torso, over which we obsess, even patronizing specialized parlours to have their respective hairs groomed and/or rent from our flesh. But who ever heard of a waxed neck? Or a neckbeard decoratively crimped at the salon?

As I awaited my fate, I catalogued my life in necks. First in fashion: before my daily apparel comprised only robes, I'd worn, variously and experimentally, turtlenecks, scoop-necks and V-necks, neckties and neckerchiefs, and even, in a brief foray into personal bejewelment, a necklace, not to mention, for several weeks after a luge mishap, both a neckwarmer and a neckbrace.

But these weren't my only neck-related follies. Facing the end, now, I began to regret my life as something of a pencil-neck who constantly relied on more brassneck-types to stick out their necks to save my neck. Had I been a millstone and albatross around the necks of everyone I'd ever known? At my funeral would the eulogies recall me as, mostly, a pain in the neck? The mere thought made the hair stand up on my neck. Yet was that fair? Growing up in an orphanage in a neck of the woods neck-deep in rednecks, with roughnecks constantly breathing down my neck, I'd made it out by the scruff of my neck. Ultimately, I thought, every life ends in a deadnecked draw between accomplishment and regret, and even if you win by a neck the best you can hope to have gotten out of the whole gooseneckeded affair is some necking, if not a broken neck.

Oh, I thought distantly, I wonder what Jerome's countdown is at?

I listened closely. And discovered only an expectant hush. There was no ominous, beeping pulse as the numbers descended on the 'ticking, timed bomb' of my fate. Flexing my earholes, I tried to achieve heightened auditory capability, as the tone-deaf pianist compensates by hammering the keys in a pugilistic rage. Would Jerome sound an alarm? Might I detect the lurch of my executioner as she moved to drop the blade? Or the murmur of the crowd as she placed her hand upon the lever? Or the shinking sound of the mechanism releasing from above?

But there was simply nothing to hear. The whole island felt like a great aural vacuum; no chirrup of birds, no shushing waves, no gurgle of bellies. Nary a breath nor a heartbeat. Nary a bloody sound.

I pictured that blade above, glinting in the obnoxious sun.

I pictured the Professor-cum-Executrix, her eyes glinting with arousal and menace.

I pictured Jerome, glinting cylindrically.

A lot of glinting, at least to the mind's eye. Yet none of it felt jovial, like the glint of the merry confectioner's gold tooth as children swarm his shop. This was much more sinister, like the glint of the razorblades with which he laces every lolly.

But then!

A gasp from the crowd.

My cue! I bucked upright and ducked to the side.

No robot pushed me back. I was safe. And still gamely capitated!

Yet, lying there on the wooden stage, I didn't hear the blade hurtling down – no telltale thunk of finality, no oohs and ahhs from the crowd at my narrow (and daring!) escape. So what was happening? Rustling, shuffling … Brad Beard protesting … And then a thwack of fist striking chin … Boards groaned as Sayer backed down the steps, begging for her life with clause upon pleading clause …

Just as I sensed a new presence in our midst, I felt hands upon me. My response was to squeal through my hood like a wrangled piglet. So here it was: shunted back under the blade to my death and doom. Off with my head! Let everyone eat cake but me.

Though, wait. I wasn't thrust forward but eased upright. These were friendly hands. Familiar. Smoothing my robes, soothing me. And off came not my head, but the hood. Standing there was my wife, Dr. Dhaliwal, dressed in her old security guard's uniform. In one hand she held the Cowl of Destiny by the Bobble of Guilt. In the other: a massive flashlight.

– Hello, she said.

Nearby, massaging his bruising temple, cowered Brad Beard and, hiding behind the still-shrouded Eye and Ewe, I spied Professor Sayer. I was about to ask after Jerome, but then noticed the column lying side-stage, tipped over and seemingly decommissioned, with a view up its innards. Inside wasn't circuitry or some digital mainframe: the fellow was as hollow as a toilet roll.

– Hollow? I asked.

– Fundamentally hollow, said my wife. But also: look.

I followed her finger. Something had rolled out of Jerome's insides – melons, I thought. Three of them. No, not melons.

Heads.

Human heads! In varying shades of green! The first, as verdant as an evergreen, had the look of oxidized bronze – identical to the ones that comprised the courtyard statue. The next was a lighter, nauseous, putrid colour, like someone seasickened inside a rotating drum, and more identifiably human, specifically female: the deadhead's eyes were closed, her lips sealed. And the final, third head, which looked freshly lopped from its body, had once crowned half of the duo previously known as Tubs and Pudding.

From the silence that swelled vaporously over the square came a sudden, desperate keening. And then this sharpened into an elegiac cry:

– Oh no, lamented the poor, forsaken widower. Oh my darling. Oh no, oh no!

Beard and Sayer launched into action, seizing heads and stuffing them back inside the fallen robot as if loading shot into a cannon. Then they righted the column, the Professor pressed the reset button – Jerome's head-screen flared angrily – and the three of them wheeled upon us. Apologetically, I hoped?

But K. Sohail urged me:

– Run!

And off she ran, and so did I.

Into the village we fled. Was anyone after us? Unclear. Though I wondered, sprinting barefoot down a narrow alley, following the squeak of K. Sohail's sneakers, if perhaps our flight might have inspired a chase. For nothing excites the predatory instincts of any animal, from human to rodent to gnat, like the thrill of pursuit. Strolling blithely out of the square, with a cordial wave goodbye, might have occasioned a less perilous getaway. Less suspicious, certainly. Yet, I thought, as we cornered into a shadowy alley, we were likely owed a comeuppance for having broken the rules of Sudden Death.

Although: were *we*?

I'd been playing 'fairly square.' It was my wife who'd knocked off and emptied Jerome of his artificially sourced intelligence. It was she, not I, who'd interrupted the trial's final act, poleaxed Brad Beard with her torch and threatened the Executrix from the stage. So while it would have been ungrateful not to appreciate being saved from almost certain decapitation and concomitant death, the situation we now found ourselves in – flight – hadn't exactly been mutually engendered. Did I feel resentment, as I ducked behind Dr. Dhaliwal through the bead-curtained doorway of some modest, hut-like domicile? Surely not; I appreciated her as cows worship the moon.

But was I still the Advocate? Or had my wife's intervention compromised my status – the only title of significance I'd ever held, short of the expected childhood sobriquets (Mothbrain, Oof, Lord Pinky Tremblesbottom, the Human Crustless Sandwich, Mr. Slurps, Case #4901G, His Royal Dryness, Botchy, Ganglor, Cap'n Gas, Tinkernuts, Little Ravi Pantaloons, the Chalkboard Surprise, Flukeboy, Poopsy Lungi, Madame Floop, Sickly McDarkheart, Slimehands, Sir Weeps-a-Lot, etc.). Maybe Brad Beard had a point: Who was I, really?

But my existential crisis would have to wait. Dr. Dhaliwal was descending a staircase to the home's basement. She waited for me at the bottom of the stairs, shining her flashlight into the dark. The beam revealed a hole in the wall, more like a mouth than a door, and a strangely meaty tunnel. Fashioned from, seemingly, musculature. Pinkish. Gooey. Sinewed. And the fleshy walls throbbed slightly, as if with some internal pulse.

In there? Really?

– Go, she cried. Go! Go! Go!

So I stumbled into her nervous halo of light and that moist, sinuous tunnel. The smells were ironic and dank, and a wheezing sound accompanied the squelch of our footsteps over the spongy, undulating floor.

– Keep going, grunted my accomplice, right behind me. It's not far.

I quickened my pace – from shuffle to scuttle, to scurry, to scoot, chasing the light from her torch. Were those nets of capillaries and veins hanging from the ceiling? Or a literal bundle of nerves? We seemed to be travelling the esophagus of some leviathan, all the way to its bowels, where a slosh of acids would dissolve the very flesh from our bones. A swift beheading seemed favourable to being digested, slowly, like a muffin or carrot.

Scoot became scamper!

– Why are you running like that? Do you need the toilet?

– No! How much further?

– Just up ahead.

– Okay! And then?

– And then we'll be there.

Irrefutable. On we went, through the humid, organic air, chasing that wiggling nimbus ... to hell? My god, is that where it lit the way? Perhaps I had died a Sudden Death after all, and the Ferryman had adopted the form of my old companion to shepherd me to the netherworld?

– There, said Dr. Dhaliwal, and I looked up.

Another door! A portal to endless torment? Or someplace better?

I paused, cupping its 'knob': a human kneecap, I was fairly certain.

– Come on!

With a deep breath, I closed my eyes, twisted the handle, pushed through, and stumbled over the threshold to wherever my fate, and friend, had brought me.

Even before my eyes adjusted to the dim lighting, an odour of hot plastic invaded my nostrils, and the whirring noise of fan-cooled circuitry assaulted my ears, and an electromagnetic prickle goosepimpled my skin, and a faintly metallic taste, as if I'd gobbled a handful of loose change, filled my mouth. All of it suggested one thing, which my vision gradually confirmed: computers.

Dr. Dhaliwal had brought us to the vault beneath the Welcome Centre where the Retreat's digital 'mothering board' ticked and hummed and kept things running. We'd previously passed through this space transitionally, and now, as my wife tracked the beam of her torch slowly around the room, I took it in with greater attention.

The floors were concrete. The exposed ceilings were knotted with wires as ropy as kudzu, which threaded down into a dozen cabinets blinking with insistent lights and humming dully. The processors seemed to vibrate with some private inner life, as if within them thrummed all the most provocative secrets of anyone who'd ever Retreated here. And perhaps they did.

For what is a computer, I thought, but an endless repository of the past? Yet, I thought, it is also, simultaneously and paradoxically, the beating heart of the present. Or even, perhaps, one step ahead of it, since a computer has long been the consummate symbol of *the future*, in all its technological potential and possibility. Computers both exist within and, per their lightspeed machinations, transcend time. More than any of our species' vain attempts to capture the chronological in some figurative sense (clocks, sundials, calendars, bedpost notches to mark the drearily passing days and/or paramours) we might think of computers as not just representing but *being* time: they operate in a fluid state of recollection and projection, circuitously and linearly, synthesizing past, present, and future into one continuous, contiguous program of read-outs, codifications, results, and responses. They exist materially alongside us, in space and time, and yet ontologically *where they happen* is virtual and attendantly atemporal.

This chronological paradox is embodied by any transcriptive account of events typed into a computer: 'now' becomes multivalent, concomitantly referring within the text to events being described (the past), to the moment of their transcription (the present), as well as the moment they will eventually be read (the future). Consider this sentence: 'At this moment, I thought, you, gentle reader, would look up from the page and think, *Why is he telling me this now?!'*

Beyond the dazzling compendium of verb tenses, this phrase also provides an exemplary conflation of time in which past (event), present (documentation), and future (reception) are expressed simultaneously in a kind of ever-now. Though any temporal distinction becomes muddied if simultaneously received and mentally logged 'for later,' as textual and/or narrational material, which projects said event into the forthcoming act of writing – while writing itself, especially writing intended for an audience, is also an act of casting blindly into the future, of communicating *toward* an imagined receiver.

Further, consider if said reader engages with the text with intimations of posterity – perhaps to boast, if the text confers intellectual status or cultural currency, or has been recommended to the reader by a loved one, or for a 'book club,' or the reader is a reviewer or critic whose intention, while reading, is to write about the text for an audience. The process then initiates another recursive spiral, as one engages with a forthcoming, anticipated moment of discussion while ostensibly reading in the putative *now*, thereby dividing one's attention between present and future and fracturing, and perhaps compromising, the more immediate phenomenology of the text.

Finally, when event, documentation, and reception are all performed with 'one eye' fixed on the ever-scrolling horizon of what-is-yet-to-come, none of a text's various stages of *now* ever truly occur. Without the attendant temporal and situational attention required to register, recount, or receive the formative event, the event becomes annihilated, since existence only occurs in (illusory) present time: the past is always a reconstruction, and the future always inherently imagined. So the event, which now never transpired, becomes, *even as it transpires*, a fabrication, and all texts, no matter how 'true' or based in fact, are, ergo, works of fiction.

I felt someone nudging me – my wife.

– Are you talking to yourself? Why are you nodding and grinning like that?

– Nothing! I replied hastily.

– We need to shut this whole thing down.

– Ah, yes. Or … ?

– What do you mean *or*? Or …

My wife made a chopping motion to the back of her neck and dropped her head as if it had detached.

– Of course, I said. So how do we stop it?

She squinted at me.

– Oh, I said. Right. The computers.

– They run everything. We need to find the plug.

– And pull it, I confirmed.

My wife stared. – Yes, she said slowly, and pull the plug.

– Well what are we waiting for! I cried. Let's find and pull the plug, lest we end up in another round of Sudden Death with no rescuer, i.e., you, to save us!

We began tracing all those cords and wires to their potential hub. From one tower of purring computations I followed a promising cable only to find it jag up the wall and through the ceiling to some output on an upper floor. So I dropped to my belly and wriggled alongside another lead across the floor – which fed into another cabinet.

– Any luck? asked my wife from the opposite side of the room.

– None, I reported, and paused, face down, to allow myself a hopeful fantasy of what transpired on the surface: the Retreaters, led by the freshly betrayed Tubbing, would have turned on Jerome, Sayer, and Beard, emptying the robot of his head-fuel, gagging Sayer, and shaving their formerly prized Solicitor right down to his striking, angular cheekbones. A shame, actually, that I wasn't up there to see it …

– Are you talking to yourself again?

– No! I jolted to all fours, like a dog scolded to attention. Have you found the plug?

– No. Keep looking.

I crawled down to the end of the cabinets, from which a bluish light trembled up the room's back wall, and squeezed into the little alley behind the circuitry. Here I discovered a bank of televisions from floor to ceiling, screens glowing ethereally, save one 'dead set' in the bottom corner. But unlike the sets in our rooms, these weren't streaming lascivious 'hardy core,' but footage of the village – specifically, hand-held shots galloping toward the exit.

The Retreaters seemed to have been driven into a kind of rampage; here was the video proof. Of rebellion? No, among their roiling masses I spied Sayer, ungagged, and Beard, looking positively ursine. So they were coming for us. Why? Perhaps for having been denied a spectacular finale. I could easily imagine the refrains of their homicidal pep rally: *The Dhaliwals must pay / For ruining this stupendous day / It's not Sudden Death / If the Advocate left / So let's find him and his mutinous so-called wife and decapitate them ourselves with whatever 'sharps' we can find and impale their heads on a broom handle and stuff the whole lot kebab-style up Jerome's rear-end.*

The televised stampede had reached the market. The screens seemed to present slightly different footage. I squinted, comparing. Ah. Each monitor relayed a subjective broadcast from a specific, individual Retreater. And from the hysterically jostling, waist-level cinematography, I gathered that the cameras were lodged in their wristbands.

Which meant that ... My god, here was a shot of that very bank of screens! I wagged my arm and watched the picture bounce. So I'd been turned into a vehicle of my own surveillance, I realized, with all the thematic nuance of a punt to the groin. I went at my wristband with my teeth, chewing the plastic with rat-like fervour until it tore free.

With relief I watched 'my' screen turn to static, then black – matching the dead one beside it, surely K. Sohail's. On the rest of them, something truly lascivious was afoot. Every member discarded their robes as they passed through the turnstiles, surging onto the jungle trail as naked as 'babes.' Upon their chests, I noticed, they all bore a strange, identical insignia, either painted there or etched into the skin.

What was it? I squinted. Some sort of cross-hatched circle. A bull's eye? No. What they'd drawn upon their bodies was a figurative call-to-arms against a common, mutinous enemy. The trial had failed and they were out for blood.

The symbol, displayed with fevered uniformity upon every member of the raging clan, was a K: crudely encircled, and exterminated with an annihilating X.

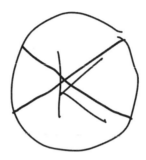

I hurled my wristband into the shadows and called K. Sohail over to have a look at what was coming for her, ergo us.

The gap between the computer cabinetry and the wall was narrow, so we had to wedge in tightly to share a decent view. Immediately my focus shifted from the footage of our would-be assailants to the proximity of our bodies: her sneaker nudging my bare foot, our knees softly knocking, her shoulder pressed to mine. At each point of contact my skin zipped and sizzled as if sprinkled with embers. Though that probably sounds torturous, like being waterboarded with yogurt. What I experienced was far more tantalizing and enlivening: an effervescent, enhanced interrogation of the soul – and heart.

Did she feel it too? I glanced over. K. Sohail watched the monitors with an intensity bordering on mania – the focused assessment and attendant strategizing of a battle-hardened warrior. But what if, like mine, her fixed, unblinking gaze actually bounced off the screens and refracted inward, as if they were mirrors for introspection?

Perhaps she was thinking what I was thinking. Being: we'd played at husband and wife, sort of. That ruse was over. Yet I felt enclosed with her inside that circled, sloppy X, and targeted together in those crosshairs of lunacy and rage. In some way, I was 'K' now too. What did that make us? Not lovers, certainly – colleagues? Allies? 'Comrades with arms'? Or something more? Something soul-matey and ... deeper?

– Look at them, she grunted. Paired up like losers.

I retracted from her touch as if stung. What a fool I'd been to insinuate myself. This was the mighty, autonomous K. Sohail, as lone as a wolf on an island on a moon in the faraway forgotten depths of the galaxy. She was nobody's anything, let alone mine.

We no longer touched. The space between us felt cold. She watched the screens: the Retreaters plunged nudely out of the jungle and up through the hammocks. She sighed and looked away. Blinked. Leaned back. Shook her head.

– This isn't good.

– No, I concurred, as that slavering, naked horde crusaded toward the Welcome Centre. In the lobby the wristband cameras captured Brad Beard and Professor Sayer organizing the unruly gang into a circle – to, it seemed, chant. There was no sound accompanying the moving pictures, so I had to lip-read.

The best I could do:

– *Gonna eat their faces / Gonna eat their ears / Gonna eat their 'places' / Gonna eat their fears / Gonna slurp their veins / Gonna chew their cud / Gonna wash it down / With a glass o' traitor-blood.*

Or perhaps:

– *Brad Beard's really barmy / And so is the Prof / Jerome's amassed an army / And we're all in the buff / All of us are clothesless / We feel so g-darn free / So very liberated / Like wingèd manatees.*

Or:

– *We painted symbols on our chests / And in certain cases between our breasts / Tubbing also has fulsome pecs / But not his husband anymore because he's basically just a bedsheet of flesh.*

Or:

– *Killing is our favourite thing / Our favourite thing, our favourite thing / Killing is our favourite thing / Besides eating eyes.*

Or:

– *There's not a murderous thing about us, none / We cheer the Advocate for a job well done / For K. the warpaint merely scrawls / 'A kiss (and hug) from the Dhaliwals!'*

No, that last one seemed delusional. Especially now that everyone dropped to their knees in seeming reverence of a skin-cloaked figure who entered the centre of the circle. Tubbing! Lording over his peers with the righteousness of a prophet. In each hand he held a bulging sack that he thrust toward the ceiling, and his disciples dropped their foreheads to the floor.

For a moment, stillness. Then Tubbing shook the bags loose to reveal their contents: two freshly severed human heads. I squinted but needn't have, for it was clear who'd ended up in the guillotine, and whose cranial offcuts were now being rolled out upon the floor. Alas, rather than stew in his sadness he'd transmuted it into rage and vindication. And here came Jerome, gliding over. He lifted at the base to vacuum up one skull, and then eased over to inhale the other. Rejuvenated, his head-screen blazed with a green checkmark. The Retreaters responded by madly genuflecting before Tubbing as if he had harvested the heads himself. Which perhaps he had.

– Oh boy, sighed K. Sohail.

She pressed her body to mine again. And not accidentally. She leaned into me in a seeking, almost dependent way. My heart, as they say, melted (not literally; in fact it thudded with firm and carnal vigour). Did we require a label? No! We were just two people who needed each other, sometimes. So I met her feet, legs, hips, waist, shoulders, and, finally, temples, with my own, conjoining with my old companion like a pair of acorns twinned upon the tree.

And like that we squatted, pressed together, side by side, sharing our mutual weight in the shuddering light of all those TVs. We watched Tubbing summon his disciples to their feet. Brad Beard and Professor Sayer moved to flank him like seconds or valets. That skin-cape struck me now as a kind of mantle, one worn for ceremonies in the darkest, most diabolical arts.

– They killed them, said my wife. Those poor people.

– Yes, I said. And it's all my fault.

– Well, she said, clutching my arm, it's all our faults. Probably.

Collective guilt! Perhaps this might allow me to escape 'as free as a Scott'? But my wife's expression had contorted into a grimace I'd never seen before. It made me sad. So as Tubbing reassembled the mob behind Jerome to push into the depths of the Welcome Centre, I took her hand in mine and squeezed.

– They're coming, said Dr. Dhaliwal.

– To eat us? I asked.

She gave me a curious look. – You think?

This was all I needed to hear. I glanced away from the screens, desperately searching the room. My gaze paused on the computer cabinetry. It had hinges. Like a door.

And, suddenly, I – of all people! – had a plan.

Around the side of the unit I found a latch and a handle. Though when I tried to haul it open, the thing wouldn't budge. Locked!

Dr. Dhaliwal scuttled forward. From her hip she produced her ring of keys and began to try one after another. On the monitors, the mob seemed to be descending to the basement, though it was hard to tell; in this spatially deranged building a down-sloping ramp could have perversely climbed to the roof. Though the Retreaters' fervour and purpose – no chanting now, simply a steely-eyed march – suggested that Jerome knew exactly where to take them. Ergo, exactly where we were.

Of course he did! Surely he was networked into the mainframe.

Meanwhile my wife tried key after key: one was too big; another too small; the next entered but wouldn't turn; this entered but twirled ineffectually. Blast!

Was there a worse fate than being consumed by a ravenous throng? Having one's flesh torn asunder, one's extremities gobbled? Witnessing one's own evisceration, the innards unravelled like garden hose? Never mind suffering the gastronomic critiques: *This breast's too dry* or *I prefer less marbled thighs* or *Such a pulpy liver* or *I can't finish this, you want the elbows?*

At least, I thought, as Dr. Dhaliwal jangled through her keyring – the castaways now outnumbering the yet-attempted – when those delirious cannibals fell upon us, she and I would perish together. Perhaps we'd even remain touching while being consumed. I glanced at the monitors: the Retreaters had reached the lower levels – pushing, as I watched, into the aviary, where the birds watched ambivalently from their perches as the naked horde surged past below.

– They're close, I reported to Dr. Dhaliwal, who sighed as another key failed. How many remained? A half-dozen at most. The next one, a copper number with serrations as drastic as shark's teeth, didn't work either. The floor quaked as the mob thundered through the basement. A minute away, perhaps less.

– Hurry, I said unnecessarily. Perhaps irritatingly. But it afforded the chance for an apology: a hand on K. Sohail's shoulder; a gentle, supportive squeeze.

Another key, another flop. The whole room shook. The Retreaters were nearly upon us. I pictured them approaching the final doglegs, gums bared, gushing drool, teeth gnashing and smashing, as wild and zealous as a pack of crazed, half-starved mules –

And then the first footsteps came slapping into earshot, which intensified into podiatric applause as, two-by-two, the group swarmed into the control room.

– They're here, whispered K. Sohail, head hanging.

And the monitors verified what we could hear and smell and fairly taste. It was true. They were there.

Despite the onslaught of Retreaters and their musky, naked funk, no one immediately checked between the supercomputer and the rear wall, where K. Sohail and I hid, snug as 'two rugged bugs.' For the moment, we were safe. So we stilled our breath, daring not try another key – their jangle would be our demise – and listened as Professor Sayer addressed the gathering.

– They've discarded their wristbands, the dastards, so Jerome's going to have to tap the Inner Net for advanced surveillance measures, and while he does that why don't we, collectively, try a final exercise, which Bradley and I are certain will prepare us, collectively, for group Trunity, to truly meld our souls as one –

– Which will – if I may, Rosie, since everyone's probably way more used to these exercises guided by my mellifluous voice – meld our souls as one. We're nearly there, folks! And I know everyone's probably like, 'Do you mean Peak Cohesion, Double-B?' Yeah, kinda. But also more than that? First what we gotta do is everyone get real close.

– Yes, everyone, please, pack in, indeed, like sardines in the tin, even you, sir, no need to be shy, nice and tight, there's plenty of room, just climb on top, or squeeze in here, that's it Tubbing, we're all your throuple now, who's to say whose hand, or thigh, is whose, and who cares, it's about sharing, about communing, about connecting …

– It's *about*, as you're no doubt familiar with if you've even skimmed any of my books, creating a Sharing Tapestry …

– To, yes, collectively, voice our frustrations, disappointments, wishes, regrets, desires, lusts, wants, needs, proclivities, tastes, so, now, yes, please, feel free to disclose whatever you'd like, it's about harmony and cohesion, please say anything you'd like …

– Anything at all. This is how it begins, folks. And how it ends.

On the video screens, two dozen-odd bodies stitched themselves atop Tubbing into a knot of flesh. Quickly it became impossible to tell where one form began and another ended. Faces crammed into armpits. What you assumed was a toenail turned out to be an eye. Was that globular hump a buttock or a kneecap? Or a chin? Or half a bosom?

– I'll go first, said a small, buried voice that might have been Tubbing. My name's –

– No names, please, rather, in our glorious nudity, let's adopt the cloak of anonymity, to, I believe, liberate us from the strictures, as well as the innate constraints, of nomenclature, and truly destroy the boundaries between each one of us, soul and body.

– Codenames are cool, though, ma'am. Wanna try again?

– Sorry, Mr. Beard. Sorry, Prof. Can I be 'Boingboing Darkstar'?

– I'm 'Guadalupe the Impaler!'

– Dang it. I wanted that one.

– Oh, you can have it. Happy to use my backup, 'Old Horker.'

– Gross.

– Not horker as in spitting!

– Folks, please, cried Brad Beard. Can we get on task? The point here is to *meld* via the sharing of secrets, not compete for naming rights. Tell us about your losses, your regrets, your failures, your shame, your humiliations, your worst times ever –

– Your pain, added Professor Sayer with surprising concision.

From here the mob unleashed a chorus of confession through which K. Sohail and I, secreted in our nook, winced in embarrassment.

– I'm cold, it began.

– I'm frightened.

– I'm into ducks in probably a dangerous way.

– Does this look like leprosy to you? Here, and here, it goes all the way around …

– Well, I'll simply say this: as a child I often wondered if the milkman was some sort of farm animal in disguise. A ewe, or a sow. Trying, perhaps, to get the inside scoop.

– Oh, I should probably tell you all that before my husband and I came here we robbed about a dozen banks, and there's a bounty on our heads across several counties in the coastal northwest. I mean, that's how we afforded to come to the Retreat, so I wouldn't take it back and regret nothing. And to be honest it was all super exciting, especially the high-speed getaways. Also I don't love my children and never have.

– At our wedding – no, it's fine, my love, everyone should know – we'd written our own vows but I mixed up the slips of paper and brought my grocery list instead, and I was so nervous I just read it without thinking, and they were really very weird groceries.

– I killed a cat as a child, I think. Possibly also nine of my classmates.

– Okay, here we go: my neighbour and I got involved in some off-brand witchcraft and accidentally swapped souls about seventeen years ago. So I'm sorry to have to tell you this, my darling, but I'm not your wife. It's me, Jeremy, from Apartment 205. You've been living a lie for nearly two decades.

– Well, that's fine … since I've been balling 'Jeremy' since the end of last century!

– Wow.

– Yeah, seriously, what are the odds?

– I mean, that one's going to be hard to top. Really compelling.

– Please, everyone, it's not a competition, the idea here, if Bradley and I failed to make ourselves clear, isn't to outdo one another, but to use our secrets to tear down the boundaries between us, to meld our souls –

– To achieve Trunity! To reach Peak Cohesion! To open the door to *the other side*!

– IN TRUTH JEROME HAS NEVER ENJOYED THIS WORK. REGARDS, JEROME.

– IN TRUTH JEROME ABHORS YOU ALL. REGARDS, JEROME.

– IN TRUTH JEROME IS ONLY HERE FOR THE HEADS. REGARDS, JEROME.

– IN TRUTH JEROME NEEDS FEEDING. FEED HIM HEADS NOW. REGARDS, JEROME.

– Jerome, please, have you accessed the Inner Net, have you found the fugitives?

(In the ensuing silence, I could easily picture the evasive ellipses scrolling across Jerome's head-screen.)

– Anyway! I write letters to mailboxes, but when I put them in the mailboxes I wonder, 'Was that too easy?'

– Is it weird that I've never liked … anyone? Literally. Ever. My husband's looking at me now like, *Oh god what is my life*, ha ha ha. Sorry, Sweetlips, but it's true.

– Since the Retreat started I haven't peed once. Not once! I have no idea what's going on. Nothing like this has ever happened before. I usually go five, six times a day. And it's not like I haven't been hydrating. I've been drinking like a – what do you call those toy birds that dip down and sip water and then swing up and then go back down, again and again? The plastic ones, red with big goofy eyes in a little yellow hat?

– Blue. The hat's blue.

– You sure? I could swear it's yellow.

– No, ma'am, you're an imbecile. It's blue. And that's nothing. For years I've been hiding that I'm actually a train. Thanks to your Sessions, Professor, and your motivation, Mr. Beard, and with my partner's encouragement I've been exploring my real identity – just chugging around, finding my tracks. Well yesterday after Stretching I tried picking up passengers for the first time, and I won't name any names but it was pretty humiliating when no one got on board. I'm not blaming anyone, just next time I pull into the station maybe consider taking a ride on the Big Boy Steam Engine Choo-Choo Express.

Brad Beard interjected again. In his supervisory capacity, I assumed. But then as he spoke a scandalous revelation emerged.

– People! Please, everyone. Just stop. Be quiet. I've been lying here with my head between the Professor's legs, listening to you all, and I can't take it anymore. It's time I confessed something. Something I've been holding on to for far too long. Oh boy. Okay, give me a moment here … Phew … Wow. This is really happening. Ready? Here we go: the beard's not real. It's not a real beard. It's not even hair. It's just steel wool and two-sided tape. You can peel the whole thing off in one go. There it is. And I know what you're all thinking: 'How can we trust anything Brad's ever told us in his lectures, seminars, concert series, and textbooks?' Which I understand. I mean this must be like finding out that God's just a guy in a fake beard or something. But listen. Think about how far we've come together. If you've learned anything from the Beard Program or Bearding, Bettering, Becoming or A Face of Beard to Face

Your Fears, it's that your real beard – your *true* beard – isn't the one you wear on your face. That can be shaved or waxed off in an instant. Or, sure, unglued. The real beard, friends? The beard that guides us, that we harbour and cherish, that's our #1 Soul-Fire? That son of a greased gun is – you guessed it: in your heart. Deep. Buried. Vast. And if you've got a beard like that, nothing can take your Trunity away from you, as long as you both shall live.

– Hold on, you're telling us what now?

– What about *the other side*?

– Yeah, Brad! What even matters anymore, sheesh!

– What matters? Well, 'sheesh,' I'd say what matters is finding those doshgarn fugitives, if anyone remembers that whole thing and isn't all suddenly caught up in who's beard's real and who's swindling whom. Any luck on that front, J-dog?

– ACCORDING TO THE INNER NET, THEY ARE ... HERE. REGARDS, JEROME.

– I'm sorry, Jerome, but, if I understand correctly, you mean to say that the imposters are, is it, here with us, in this very room?

– YES, ALONG WITH THEIR NOURISHING HEADS, PLEASE. REGARDS, JEROME.

– Creepy!

– Ew!

– Yeah, what are we even doing anymore?

– Let's freaking get them!

I watched with horror as the bodies across that bank of screens began untwining to resume their hunt. Yet one monitor remained motionless. As everyone climbed off him and dispersed around the room, Tubbing was left lying on the floor; he must have had his hands cupped in front of his face so the wristband captured it in close-up. And what a face. He looked so tired.

I reached out to caress his cheek (virtually). Stunningly my fingers encountered not the hard glass of a TV screen, but a sort of jellied membrane. I recoiled with a gasp.

K. Sohail frowned and reached out to touch the same screen. Her finger passed through Tubbing's unblinking eye, right to the knuckle. And then her whole hand was swallowed, followed by her arm, right up to the shoulder.

On the rest of the screens Retreaters shuffled around the room. The air crackled with blood lust as they fanned out in couples, on the prowl, the symbol on their chests smeared from the orgiastic pile-on. It was only a matter of moments before someone peeked behind the computers. We were doomed!

Yet K. Sohail had both arms sunk into Tubbing's monitor. She swivelled her head at me with a look of resignation.

– I'm going in. Will you come?

Voices and footsteps approached the back of the cabinets. On the other screens I could see Retreaters coming our way. I felt breath gusting from around the corner. I could smell, for some reason, the sea. Our discovery was imminent. And then there was Tubbing, or his televised self, providing us a way out.

I nodded at K. Sohail.

– See you on the other side, she said. And then she launched herself fully into Tubbing's pixelated face.

I watched her whole body slip inside the screen, her sneakers wiggling – and then she was gone. All that remained was Tubbing, his mouth opening to swallow me whole.

– There he is, I heard someone shout. The so-called Advocate!

– He's all alone again like a weirdo!

– Let's get him.

Bodies came hurtling into the little alley between the monitors and wall. Hands clawed at my robes. Teeth gnawed my ankle.

It was, as they say, 'nohow or never.'

So I dove into the screen, after K. Sohail, and for a moment all I saw was light.

From light came light. And then there was light.

– What? Said K. Sohail.

I'd been narrating aloud, apparently.

– Just spitting balls, I confessed.

– What?

– Ball-spitting?

– Spitballing?

– *Spitballing*, yes!

– We barely escaped being eaten alive. And you're ... spitballing.

– Spitballing, I declared proudly. I could have clutched her, this scholar and gentlewoman, who, with one pedantic clarification, had anointed me an idiomatic king!

After a heavy, long, beleaguered sigh, she spoke again: – Can you see anything?

– Yes.

– You can? Really? What?

– What can I see?

– Yes. I can't see anything. What's out there?

– Light.

– No. No, no ... Good lord. *Other* than light.

– Oh. Not really?

– Nothing, then.

– Other than light? No, nothing.

– Great. Give me your hand?

– My ... oh, okay! Wow! Okay. Are we ... *holding hands*?

– Just don't let go.

– Certainly not!

– Don't let go, okay?

– I won't.

– Good?

– Good. Okay.

– Should we ... walk?

I was taken aback, momentarily, that this Woman of Action – and Virtuoso of Rhetoric – would seek my counsel on anything, let alone our next move. I peered into all that whiteness. Yet our surroundings weren't something one could look *at*, exactly: the void simply expanded in every direction, all around us, forever.

– Forward? I asked.

– Ideally, she said.

– We could ... try?

And so we did. Careful, small steps, hand in hand. If walls or a ceiling framed this chamber of light I couldn't see them. If we were outdoors, no horizon loomed ahead. Nothing marked our progress. This was like strolling on an invisible treadmill inside the blank mind of a catatonic. Yet K. Sohail's hand was warm in mine, and it was good to hold on to someone amid that colourless oblivion.

Beyond each other, the only companion to our tentative march was a distant, obstinate drone. As we proceeded, this fractured into a low growl that rumbled in the deeper bass registers and then a second note, high above it, emerged in harmony: a shrill, needling whine so barely audible it seemed to whistle at the edge of perception. And then the two notes conjoined into another, fuller monotone hum.

We'd walked for five minutes or so, though without any landmarks to gauge our progress, we seemed to merely shuffle in place. K. Sohail looked behind us, ahead, to the sides, and up and down. As did I.

– We're not getting anywhere, she said.

– It would seem not, I agreed.

– Though maybe we are?

– Yes! I think so!

She stopped moving, let go of my hand – abandonment! – and turned her eyes upon me. A look of scrutiny and appraisal? No. She was simply using me as a 'board of sound' upon which to nail her gaze so she could think. I wasn't sure what to do with my face. A garrulous grimace? A fandangled frown? A snootling … snoot?

– Stop that. You look like you're having a stroke.

I tried to ease my expression into neutrality. Flat mouth. Calm ears. Dead eyes. The eyes of the dead! A dead man's gape!

– All right, she said, and removed the ring of keys from her hip, undid the clasp, and laid a key on the ground.

– Ah, I said. A 'key party!'

But when I knelt to gather it, she pulled me upright by the scruff of my robes.

– A cairn, in fact, she clarified.

K. Sohail held out her hand. I slid mine into it. Yet when I tried to interlace fingers she gently rejected the move and re-established a more cordial grip.

We began walking again. And after twenty paces stopped to look back. The key had receded. Or, rather, we had left it behind.

– So we *are* getting somewhere, she said, and dropped another key at our feet.

We proceeded another ten yards and checked: the second key sat starkly in our wake; the first had shrunk to a silver blemish amid all that white.

– I guess we keep going? she said.

– Tally your hoes! I screamed.

She dropped another key, and on we went, stopping at greater intervals to check, and leave another, until she stopped after the six or seventh key.

– This is stupid. I'm just leaving a trail for them to follow.

– A crumby trail, I agreed.

We listened. The drone had changed pitches. It settled into, I believe, a major third (possibly an A-natural and F-natural, though my ear is far from a maestro's). It sounded more insistent now, swelling with ardour and urgency. I thought of a mouth, opening. I thought of teeth. I thought of being lapped by slug-like tongues. I pictured wet, jabbering lips clamping over my own – the classic 'amuse-bouche.'

Meanwhile the tone crescendo'd. Deafening now, as fervent as a hymn. And closer, seemingly, though nothing visible stirred the snow-blind abyss. Was something or someone nearly upon us? I squinted, peered, observed nothing but brightness and desolation. Could whatever approached be imperceptible to the naked human eye?

Enough thought! My cheekbones hummed and my vision blurred as the reverberations boomed through my body. Something, certainly, was closing in.

– Let's move, said K. Sohail.

We linked hands. Squeezed. And took off, running.

As we ran the sound grew still louder, a behemoth's mating call that resounded through my face and hands and bones. Yet I was also becoming convinced that we were not being tracked through the void. Rather than galloping at our heels, the tone seemed to emerge ambiently from the atmosphere all around. A glance behind us confirmed it: nothing disturbed our path of discarded keys, which resembled the dotted guide-line for a colossal scissors to clip this vacant realm in two.

K. Sohail, following my gaze, appeared to agree (about the lack of pursuers; I'm not sure if the scissors analogy occurred to her). Our pace slowed – to a canter, to a trot. Finally we stopped and, standing side by side and panting (me: heavily; her: not really, actually), listened.

And the tone quieted, just like that.

Yet the sudden silence felt barren and menacing, a false refuge before some raging sonic storm. Then a new sound irrupted into the space: not a drone, this time, but a melody. Ten quarter notes lilting up and down an oddly configured scale, each one a kind of bleating pulse. And upon the completion of this little jingle, the air seemed to crystallize, as if the music were manifesting physically. The vacuum pixelated into millions – billions? trillions?! – of coloured specks, like raindrops freezing mid-fall. Yet it wasn't rain or sleet or some misty cyclone. Or even a gale of gnats to exsanguinate us dry. I squinted. No. These really were just little variegated particles, hovering in the air – or, more so, that *were* the air.

A distorted shriek fractured the quiet. This extended and lifted into a hysterical echo blaring an octave higher, while the atmosphere continued to transmogrify into more and more multicoloured specks. And then, after a few seconds of holding its highest note, that infernal soundtrack descended again into a deliriously chirruping triad, like bird-song but garbled and choked. From this trilled a scream as jagged and sinister as a razor-tipped talon carving pentagrams into the windows of a cathedral.

Another pause. As if the players of these ungodly phrases were gathering their breath. So we too breathed, watching the spots assemble anon. (I mean, of course we *breathed*, as we'd been breathing for the duration of this entire account; I've just not felt the need to narrate our every in- and exhalation.) Now, however, our respiration assumed melodramatic scope: in we gulped courage, out we blew dread and fatigue. Meanwhile that pointillist array appeared to be forming … a grid, was it?

And then everything exploded into static.

A deafening rumble thundered down upon us from all sides, tidal and cataclysmic. K. Sohail and I fell to our knees, not only covering our ears but closing our eyes, should they too permit that howling tempest to invade and colonize our brains. But this at best dampened the sound as it engulfed us.

In those supine positions we cowered, crushed, while the aural storm surged, roaring, and wracked our bodies with wave upon wave of its pain – the cries of a cyborg drowned in lava, or a man watching his favourite sandwich flushed away by the police.

– What's happening? I shouted.

– Something, yelled K. Sohail, accurately enough.

The void's orchestrations seemed to be escalating. What would be their climax? Our bones splintered to dust? Our eyeballs bursting like pin-stuck bubbles? The roaring sharpened into screams and yelps and honks and guttural bellowing, heightening in tension and torturousness, and then reassembling again for a virtuosic, terrible finale.

Cringing beneath this ferocious snarling, I felt that this was the end – not just of that auditory holocaust, but ourselves. The sound was so intense that another minute of its percussions would surely rattle our organs loose and pulverize them to goop. How wretched and pathetic to perish, audially impaled and imploded, in this aggressively illumined – and now weirdly pixelating – void. What a sad, unbeautiful corpse I'd leave, cursed to eternal rest in nothing but borrowed robes. At least K. Sohail would die in uniform! Anyone encountering our remains would recognize at once who and what she was: a woman of honour and dutiful protection – and security. My skeleton would suggest a nincompoop. Especially if the forensic rumours are true and death throes do indeed flush the bowels.

I felt a hand on my back. I freed my ears, opened my eyes. The sound was … gone. A new silence prevailed. One that didn't portend new menace, but which felt liberated and cleansed. And a face, like a moon peeking out from cloudcover, dipped into my vision. K. Sohail. And when she spoke I detected a lift to her voice. Was it hope?

– Look.

I sat up and obeyed. Those dots in the air had formed into minuscule cubes. Floating everywhere, soundless and glittering. The air was leaden with them. Or, again: they were the air. Or the atmosphere. Molecular. Pure colour. Our bodies displaced them, but beyond us they sparkled, jewel-like, and filled the space like water.

– Look closer, said K. Sohail. We've reached the Inner Net.

With mounting intensity, I focused on the cube only inches from my face. It looked about the size of a pinprick, yet the more attention I trained upon it, the more it seemed to grow – from speck to stamp-sized, to a block as big as a book, then bigger than a table, swelling further and more until I felt dwarfed and consumed.

Perhaps you have approached a television set until the image begins to diffuse and fracture? This was the opposite; the cube's contents turned more coherent as it engulfed me. It was a screen, dancing with pictures; it was a window to the promised land. It was a door, opening, to something infinitely bigger and better than me.

Finally that glowing portal swallowed my body whole, and I swam into its kaleidoscope of reds and golds and blues and pinks and greens, of crystallized shadow and liquid light, of positive and negative space. Yet I had no body here. I was just pure experience, energy, sensation – at one, I knew, with everything.

Progressively details emerged. Shades became shapes, then objects, and then the boundaries and angles of a physical plane. A room. No: a warehouse, with innumerable rows of shelving that soared from the floor to the ceiling hundreds, perhaps thousands, of feet above. The scene sharpened further into focus: the shelves were piled with cardboard boxes in all shapes and sizes – millions of them. A nation-sized stockroom of the gods.

The scene animated – from photograph to film – palpitating with movement, with life. There were people here too. Shoppers strolled the aisles piloting carts the size of cargo vans, each one loaded with purchases; employees ascended motorized lifts to fetch packages from the highest racks. Everyone was smiling. Everyone was happy.

And, gradually, I felt myself materializing among them, my vague perceptions concretizing into awareness and experience, and then flesh.

I felt my body taking shape, assuming corporeal proportions, as I was metaphysically birthed into this place. I watched my arms form and hands emerge. I felt a heart beating in my chest. And finally my bare feet, at last, settled upon the concrete floor.

All around me buzzed the expectant and anticipatory vigour of retail, the air fairly sizzling with desires and their attendant guarantees of fulfillment. A family pushed past, their cart heaped with packages, grinning from ear to ear. Their joy washed over and through me – and left me smiling too. In awe I admired the amazonian majesty of my surroundings. Everywhere were *things*. Things to be had. Things to own. Things that would become essential to realizing whatever we imagined ourselves to be.

Anything we could imagine. Everything. The world and all that was in it.

Whether this paradise was only a fantasy or a dream seemed irrelevant. I was *somewhere* now, a part of it – and no longer apart. Like everyone else here, I'd become who I was, fundamentally, in true unity with my singular, promised self. I'd never be wrong again! For in the Inner Net's utopia, I, the customer, was always right. I gripped the handles of a shopping cart, my chariot and steed, and looked around at the shelves, teeming and towering above, and felt affirmed, and determined, and full of hope.

It no longer mattered that I was alone. This place of limitless possibility, this Inner Net, was more real and sure and truthful, and made me more myself, than anyone I'd ever known, and anywhere I'd ever been.

Pasha Malla is the author of a short story collection, *The Withdrawal Method*, three books of poems, *All Our Grandfathers are Ghosts, Why We Fight > Quran Neck*, and *Erratic Fire, Erratic Passion* (with Jeff Parker), and the novels *People Park, Fugue States,* and *Kill the Mall.* He lives in Hamilton, Ontario, and teaches in the creative writing program at York University.

Typeset in Albertina and Optima.

Printed at the Coach House on bpNichol Lane in Toronto, Ontario, on Zephyr
Antique Laid paper, which was manufactured, acid-free, in Saint-Jérôme, Quebec,
from second-growth forests. This book was printed with vegetable-based ink on
a 1973 Heidelberg KORD offset litho press. Its pages were folded on a Baumfolder,
gathered by hand, bound on a Sulby Auto-Minabinda, and trimmed on a Polar
single-knife cutter.

Coach House is located in Toronto, which is on the traditional territory of many
nations, including the Mississaugas of the Credit, the Anishnabeg, the Chippewa,
the Haudenosaunee, and the Wendat peoples, and is now home to many diverse
First Nations, Inuit, and Métis peoples. We acknowledge that Toronto is covered
by Treaty 13 with the Mississaugas of the Credit. We are grateful to live and work
on this land.

Edited by Alana Wilcox
Cover design by Ingrid Paulson
Interior design by Crystal Sikma
Author photo by Vanessa Oliver

Coach House Books
80 bpNichol Lane
Toronto ON M5S 3J4
Canada

mail@chbooks.com
www.chbooks.com